SURE
SIGNS OF
CRAZY

SURE SIGNS OF CRAZY

KAREN HARRINGTON

SCHOLASTIC INC.

ISBN 978-0-545-69804-7

12 11 10 9 8 7 6 5 4 3   14 15 16 17 18 19/0

Printed in the U.S.A.   40

First Scholastic printing, January 2014

All definitions from http://dictionary.reference.com/

For the extraordinary Gigi and Lauren

chapter 1

You've never met anyone like me. Unless, of course, you've met someone who survived her mother trying to drown her and now lives with an alcoholic father. If there are other people like this, I want to meet them pronto. *Pronto*, which is my current favorite word, is what they say in cop shows when a detective wants information fast. There would be a lot I could learn from those people, especially if they are older than me, which is almost twelve. As it is right now, I have to learn most things on my own.

This is what I've written in my *real* diary. I could never say this out loud. Never.

❧

If you want to know, I have a real diary and a fake diary. The fake diary is the decoy, the one you hide in plain sight. If someone finds it and reads it, he will think you are normal and move right along. When you write in it, all you have to do is pretend an adult is reading it and say something like:

This was a great day. I got an A on the Math test, and I met a new friend named Denise, who hums during Algebra.

The real diary is just for me. Private and true. Lately, I've been writing about problems I'm trying to work out. Here's what I've written:

There are two weeks of school left. As soon as the final bell rings, I'll have two giant problems.
Problem 1: I'll have a boring summer and be forced to stay at my grandparents' boring house.
Problem 2: I'll have to go to seventh grade in three months and be forced to do that horrible Family Tree Project that Lisa's sister had to do this year. Everyone at school will know about my mother.
I can try to change Problem 1, but Problem 2 is tragically unsolvable. I can't figure out any way to

get around doing the project unless I move away
and go to another school. Investigate this option.

It's a little bit difficult to keep two diaries going, but it is necessary. I have to keep facts, clues, and lists of words where no one will see them but me. Not every person responds to words the same way. Some words are trouble words. A trouble word will change the face of the person you say it to. *Love* can be a trouble word for some people. *Crazy* is also a trouble word.

I should know.

Once, when we had just moved to Garland, into our ugly, brown rent-house on Yale Court, my dad had tensed up like he might hit something when I'd used the word *crazy* to describe my mother. It was because of career day at school. Dad had asked me if I had any idea what I wanted to be. To be honest, I had still been thinking about it because I was waiting to see if I turned out crazy like her.

So I said to Dad, "Why not wait until you figure out if you are going to inherit crazy before you decide on an occupation?" I don't know why I said this out loud. I'm usually careful with words.

I saw a hurt in Dad's eyes that made me want to leave the room. But because he was blocking the only way out of our U-shaped kitchen, there was no place to go. My backup plan was to climb inside a kitchen cabinet and hide. That is saying a lot when you think how rent-house cabinets are the most disgusting things you will ever see. If there is a list of grossest places on earth, these cabinets are on it.

"I'm sorry," I said.

He took a deep breath and told me no, I wasn't going to be crazy and please don't ever, *EVER*, use that word to describe her again, young lady! I couldn't say anything back, because I was afraid. I wish I'd had enough guts to tell him I'd looked up *crazy* in the dictionary.

I knew I'd chosen the right word.

crazy *adj.*: mentally deranged; demented; insane

I added *crazy* to my list of trouble words.

I hide the real diary between two folded towels under my bathroom sink and leave the decoy on my nightstand. It has a shiny gold lock on it, so you think it's hiding important words.

chapter 2

I was only two when my mother filled the kitchen sink with water and tried to drown me. Sometimes it feels like she was the mother of some family across the street and we watched her story on the news thinking, *Wow, too bad for that poor family.* The counselors my dad once sent me to spent all their time trying to pry details out or put details into my brain about what they called "the incident."

One of the counselors, Dr. Madrigal, was so sure I could remember some detail about that day, he asked me constantly if I had nightmares about water or a fear of water. No, I don't. But I tell you, if I'd gone to his office much longer, I'm pretty certain I'd have developed a fear of swimming.

So even though I'm her daughter and she tried to kill me, I know the story only from what's written in black and white. You would think I was an investigator. Many of the details are available to anyone with a computer. I'm scared to look up anything at home, so I've conducted my investigation at the library, using the search terms *Jane Nelson trial*.

Jane Nelson is my mother.

If you do this search, Google will tell you "there are about 821,000 results." That is how famous her case is on the Internet. You can click on her Wikipedia page first and learn simple facts. Jane Nelson was born in Texas. Her mother was killed when she was nine. Raised by her father. Went to nursing school. Became a mother at thirty-one. Committed to a mental hospital at thirty-five.

You can also click on articles about her trial and find details you wish weren't true, such as:

JANE NELSON TURNED ON THE WATER AFTER HER HUSBAND, TOM NELSON, LEFT FOR WORK.

She drowned me first. Then Simon, my older brother. He is my twin, born three and a half minutes before me. A UPS deliveryman came to the door and found my mother dripping wet. She asked him to call 911. The rest of the story is all about court cases and who was right and who was wrong and proving she was crazy.

I don't understand a lot about the trials. And, yes, I mean trials.

There were two.

First, my mother's, which led to a plea of insanity and a sentence of undetermined length at a mental-health facility here in Texas. Second, my dad's for failing to protect us. Don't ask me how to explain this since he was at work when my mother became a criminal, and of course he would've protected us. Still, the newspapers didn't write nice things about him, even after he was found not guilty.

The only thing I know for certain is that Simon wasn't as lucky as I was. He is dead in a tiny grave in Houston, and I'm in this ugly, brown house in Garland with a shiny pink cell phone making the *Crazy Frog* sound, which is how I know it's Lisa calling.

I put my diary to the side.

"Hey."

"Did you see?"

"See what?"

"Emma Rodriguez is officially in a relationship."

If you want to know, Lisa is obsessed with relationships.

"With who?" I ask.

"Go look and call me back."

"Just tell me, already."

"Go look!"

When we hang up, there is a cloud of annoyance all over me. This is what she does. Tease people with

7

information. It would be nice if I could talk to her about real things.

Like Simon.

Dr. Madrigal said I should try "sharing my feelings" with kids my age, but what does he know? He always reminded me that my mother's crimes weren't my fault. Well, I figured that out on my own, thank you very much. My mother didn't know me the way a person really knows a person. She was sick and I was only two. You would think this all doesn't matter, because it happened a long time ago, but that is not the case. News reporters like to keep reminding people about our business.

When there is a new story about a woman killing her child, there is almost always some reference to my mother. Her story is that famous.

So you can see why I am dreading seventh grade with a capital *D*. It's simply impossible to imagine myself presenting a Family Tree Project with names, details, charts, major historic events in your family, and "what is the most interesting connection you see across the generations."

Lisa's sister did the project last year, and all Lisa talked about, besides how she'd steal her sister's project and not have to do one, was how her grandmother once sang on Broadway. Lisa said that was why she was going to get the lead part in *Guys and Dolls*, which she did, so there was no shutting her up.

Of course, I could lie and make up a whole family with nice qualities like a talent for woodworking. I could say, *Oh, my family made bookshelves for George Washington, and look at this pencil I just carved.*

But I would still have to be around all these braggers like Lisa who have something good to look forward to, and my neck would turn red when I lied anyway. Especially if I have to present before fancy-dresser Angela Nee. Angela and I are side by side in the school yearbook, but that's pretty much the only time we'll ever be together on anything.

Angela Nee: Tall and green-eyed. Perfect shiny black hair. Often mistaken for a model. Raises hand in class with correct answers.

Sarah Nelson: Short and brown-eyed. Short brown hair in need of style. Often mistaken for a fifth grader. Must be called on to answer.

Maybe I don't want to be a seventh grader with a Family Tree Project that informs the world that a crazy gene runs in my family, but wouldn't I like to know a few more things about my mother? Yes, I would. I would like to get information about her and have it all to myself. Like maybe we are both good with plants. Maybe we can both make them bloom, no problem.

chapter 3

It turns out that Emma Rodriguez is in a relationship with Jimmy Leighton. That is why Lisa teased me. She knows I like Jimmy. Well.

After I finish writing about Problems 1 and 2 in my diary, I count up the days until school is out for the summer. Thirteen more days of sixth grade, including the weekend. Lisa is going to camp as soon as school lets out, so "sharing my feelings" with her is no good.

So I write down that what I need is an informant, which is a word I found in the dictionary one night.

informant *n*.: a person who supplies data in answer to the questions of an investigator

If you want to know, the pages of my dictionary are rubbed soft. I have favorite words highlighted in blue. Dad hates how I write inside books, but I love words of all sorts, and this is what I must do.

Dad should be my chief informant. But an informant talks, and he does not like to talk about anything but what he needs to pick up at the store.

This is an example of a conversation with my dad: "Are we out of milk? Cereal? How about I make pancakes on Saturday?"

In his conversations, your own input is not really required. I have to pry *real* information out of him. He is hard, frozen ice cream and I am a weak spoon. What I've learned is this: You don't get much ice cream for all the hard work you put in, and the spoon ends up bent.

Like always, I have to figure out things on my own and answer the questions my brain creates. If you want to know, I am looking for any signs of going crazy. The more information I gather, the better I can defend myself against the world, against the brain inside me that may or may not be like hers.

So far, I've decided only one thing about how to solve the problem of going to seventh grade. I will be on the case, as they say in crime shows. I will look for clues myself. I decide to write the names of all the people who know more about my mother than I do. They could be my sources. Dad, my grandparents. And, of course, my mother herself. When I get enough information, I will know what to do.

Under my dad's name, I make a note that he doesn't always tell the truth.

1. Unreliable source
2. Tells people he's a widower

Next, there are my grandparents. I write their names on a new page, make some notes about clues they might offer.

1. Besides Dad, they are the only people I know who knew my mother before "the incident."
2. My grandmother called her bohemian once.

bohemian *n.*: a person, as an artist or writer, who lives and acts free of regard for conventional rules and practices

Her tone didn't make it sound complimentary. It was the same way I sometimes tell Lisa her outfit looks "fine" when it's clearly a disaster.

On another diary page, I write my mother's name. I stare at it for a long time.

Jane Nelson.

The page stays blank.

I wish I could just walk up and ask (the way my English teacher does), *"Please, in your own words, tell me what happened the day you tried to kill me."* But I can't. I close my diary and put it back in its hiding place between the towels. Then I stare into the mirror until my eyes are like those of a person who is calm and not at all scared. I say to myself, *I want to know, in your own words, what happened. Before you answer, know that I will not hold a grudge. I'm just conducting an interview. Your cooperation is appreciated.*

I rehearse lines in front of Plant, which, if you read my real diary, you would know for sure is my best friend. There are only two things we've had at *every* rental house: Plant and the miscellaneous box. I take Plant inside the new house, and Dad leaves the miscellaneous box in the garage. When I asked him about the box, he said *miscellaneous* is stuff you don't know you need until you see it.

Most days when I water Plant, I have a new trouble word to tell her. All of them are mixed deep in her soil. If secrets were seeds, she could bloom leaves that would make me blush.

And if she did bloom and show the world all my secrets, I just don't know what I'd do. Probably lie and say, "Oh, she was here when we moved in. These are the secrets of another girl."

chapter 4

Plant agrees with me. We'll start our investigation as soon as school is out. For now, I'm suffering through a hot Saturday afternoon with the knowledge that Jimmy Leighton is in a relationship.

I officially hate this day.

Now, I try not to use the word *hate*. One of the reasons I like watching *The Rifleman* on TV is that the cowboy Lucas McCain always says stuff like "Hate is too strong a word to use just because you don't agree with someone." But if it is only one day before your twelfth birthday, this should be a fun day where you get to go to the mall and pick out your birthday present.

Well, Dad trashed that plan when he decided to hang out with Jim Beam and get drunk. This is not unusual. When he is sober, he is the Secret Service. But put a drink in him and I am on my own. So sorry, Lucas McCain, aka Rifleman, but I still hate this day.

Dad hides the Jim Beam in a Dr Pepper bottle, but I still know. And when he drinks, it is almost always because of my mother. Well, didn't I see this coming? My birthday makes him sad. My birthday is never fun for him, so I should have known not to get my hopes up about the mall.

Of course, my birthday is Simon's birthday, too, which is one clue about why my dad doesn't like to celebrate. Or it *would* be his birthday. We talk about Simon even less than we do about my mother. His name is a trouble word times ten.

It makes me sad to wonder what he would want at the mall for his birthday. When I see things boys my age have, I sometimes stop and think, *Would Simon like that? Would he want to read this kind of book? Would we be doing the same things?* Since I don't know for sure, I give him imaginary presents. This year I gave him a motor-powered scooter with blinking lights and night-vision goggles. Last year I got him a boomerang and *The Dangerous Book for Boys*, which I've read several times (especially the parts about girls). Simon suggested this book to me in a dream. We both thought it was good.

Yes, I talk to my dead twin brother sometimes. This is a sure sign I am going to turn out crazy, but who am I supposed to talk to about some things? Besides Plant, he is probably the one who knows me best.

Sarah's confidants = one living green organism and one dead brother.

Dr. Madrigal once told me it's better to think of how things really are and not how things should be, but you can't always control your imagination. Lately, I imagine the way it would be if my mother were here. I could fill up a blank page in my diary with how it should be. We wouldn't live in a dead-end cul-de-sac, staring at gray ground and listening to that annoying dog barking and clawing at the chain-link fence. My hair would be long and braided, and my clothes would be folded fresh from the dryer. If you want to know, my hair has never been braided, and most days I pull a clean, wrinkled shirt from the laundry basket.

"How about we go to the mall?" Dad had asked, pressing a hand to my shoulder, his breath already tinted with Jim Beam.

"Sure," I told him.

But then he sat on the couch and watched Westerns or whatever crime shows he had recorded. Watching shows is one of his favorite things to do, so I guess that's the only thing we have in common. But watching too many shows is another sign he's unhappy.

I told him that I was going to go outside and that he should let me know when he was ready to go to the mall. He winked at me, which gave me doubts about our plan. What usually happens when he gets that look is he falls asleep for hours. I hoped this wouldn't be the case this time, because I'd already decided we would go to Claire's and then to the iPod store. I wanted a green iPod Shuffle to listen to when I walk home from school and a gift card from Claire's. Lisa and I planned to spend it next week-end, because who wants their dad following them around a store when they are trying to pick out a purple purse or black bracelets?

Plus, even though Lisa can be a fashion disaster, she knows more than I do about coordinating accessories. She has probably twenty pairs of shoes and gives me her old ones. If it weren't for Lisa, I would have only tennis shoes and one nice pair of shoes for special events that are usually grandparent-related, so they hardly ever get worn and they don't fit me. Lisa gave me colorful flip-flops so I won't be a complete dork.

Maybe I'm a bad person because I still want a present today. While Dad is passed out, I steal twenty dollars from his wallet. Why should I have to stay home all day? I take myself for a walk to Walgreens, which is just a block or so and one major stoplight from our house. Let him worry when he wakes up, I say. Let him feel bad enough he'll let me get my ears pierced. I'm practically the only twelve-year-old I know with unaccessorized ears.

I spend almost two hours at Walgreens, sipping a Coke and reading magazines until a store employee suggests in a not-so-nice way that the store is not a library and to buy something or move on. So I buy a king-size bag of M&M'S and a paperback romance called *The Valiant Rake*. I want to know how a rake can be valiant. At the checkout counter, the mean clerk eyeballs me when he scans the book.

I also buy a black headband with a line of fake diamonds running through the center. Lisa said this would be the perfect accessory for someone with brown hair brushing the shoulders, which is what I have.

With my phone, I take a picture of myself wearing the headband and send it to Lisa.

She sends one right back of herself, showing off her sparkly blue earrings, and this message:

Fix ur ears.

Well.

I reply to her, **did you forget it's my birthday 2moro?**

She replies with a smiley face.

There's nothing I can do about my ears. My dad thinks pierced ears are for grown women only, but what does he know about fashion? Most days I have to check his socks to see if they even match, or cut off little strings dangling from his pants pockets.

When I get back from Walgreens, nothing has changed in my cul-de-sac. The cicadas are still making their rattle-snake hiss in the trees, and it's so hot you sweat standing still. At least now my hair is accessorized with some new pizzazz, which is my current favorite word. It might be the only word I know with four *z*'s.

pizzazz *n.*: attractive style; dash; flair

The only new thing here is the Sanchez Lawn Service at Mr. Gustafson's house. Mr. Gustafson is the one neighbor on the block who doesn't mow his own grass. I suppose it's because he is so bent he's starting to take on the shape of a candy cane.

The lawn crew probably doesn't care for an audience, but I walk over to Mr. Gustafson's anyway. A Mexican boy with a red cap starts his work. He doesn't look much older than I am, and I wonder how he already knows how to turn a yard into an even, green carpet with vacuum tracks on it. Why doesn't he try different patterns, give the yard alien-crop-circle swirls? As sometimes happens with me, my brain is thinking so much it forgets to tell my body to keep moving.

I stand still until the boy makes a coughing sound like I am in the way, which, as it turns out, I am.

"Oh, sorry," I say, stepping out of his way. "So, do you like this work? Mowing lawns fun?"

"No hablo inglés."

"What? Oh. I get it."

It's not that I haven't been around non-English-speaking people before. I'm not from Mars, after all. But just now, this boy in front of me and his inability to understand me are a newfound treasure. I could say anything.

"Rainbow chocolate cake winter snow porch."

He nods as if I've made perfect sense, speaking fluent alien babble. His shoes are old and grass-stained, which makes me wonder how many houses he gets to see. It must be fun to have this job. You get to work outside and see something new all the time. In my diary, I will write this down as a possible career opportunity. It would be fun to see so many different neighborhoods. I bet I could pick out the rent-houses fast. They are brown, have the most weeds, and, like our house, usually have a dead tree stump in the front yard. There is a house like this a block from here, and the people put a potted plant on their tree stump like that would dress it up. I want to kidnap that plant because she is probably going to die of embarrassment up there.

The boy with the red cap stands there, waiting to see if

I'm going to speak. Just saying secrets out loud can make you feel better, which is what I've learned from talking to Plant. She is not a person, but she is a living thing, so I know she hears me.

I begin.

"I've never French-kissed a boy," I say to him as he removes a leaf blower from the truck.

That's one.

"My dad let me drive the car once."

Two. Okay, he is still standing in front of me.

And then I wait and take a deep breath. When someone learns we are *that* family and my mother is *that* woman and I am *that* girl, we move. But just now, the want to say it is almost overpowering.

If I told you my name, you could search me on the computer and, along with a tiny mention of my twin, Simon, there I would be, the daughter of that woman. The crazy woman's daughter.

The boy moves his head to the side and squints like I've turned a flashlight on him. He starts up the leaf blower, walking around me to finish his work.

I could tell him that, but I've said enough for one day. I stand on the curb, munching my almost-melted M&M'S, and watch him make the sidewalk clean and new. The two other men on the crew load their equipment and open Gatorades and sit on the tailgate of their red truck. One of them says something that makes the other laugh and makes me wish I knew a little *español*, which I don't.

"Well, you do nice work," I say. The boy with the red cap, who is busy adjusting something on the blower, glances at me again. So I point to the grass, give him a thumbs-up, seeing how it must be a universal sign of approval. He nods.

"Cool, then. See you 'round," I say.

I walk the full circle of the cul-de-sac and wave at the lawn crew as it drives away, wondering what questions he might have asked me if he understood English, what secrets he might have. As much as I don't like nosy people, I love to know a juicy secret, too.

chapter 5

This may be the longest afternoon in the history of afternoons. My dad is still drunk.

I peeked inside the screen door, and, sure enough, he was sprawled on the couch, one hand hanging over the cushion, the other across his forehead like he got bad news and froze.

It's too far and too hot to walk to the library right now, so I'm stuck here in my own front yard with *The Valiant Rake* and melted M&M'S and nothing new to add to my knowledge of the world. I could already write a book on what I know of this stupid town. I filled a whole diary chapter about it in case I am famous and need to write my memoirs someday. Ha-ha!

We live in a neighborhood where all the streets are named after famous colleges. You'd think this signals we live in a fancy place, but no, we don't. It is the opposite of fancy. I doubt most people here even went to college. Lisa's mama says all people are part of Christ's body, so some people have to be the armpits. She says Garland is the hardworking armpit of the Lone Star State. It's a necessary body part, but it's not pretty and can be smelly, especially if you are downwind from the wastewater treatment plant, which we are. Not counting overgrown trees with middles chopped out so power lines can run through them, there's not a lot of nature here, if that's what you like, but the people are nice and they'll smile at you for no particular reason.

If my dad and I were the kind of family who stood out on our front lawns making friends with the paperboy or waving across the street as we watered our plants, we'd know plenty of interesting people. But we are not waterers. We don't even get the paper. We know who our neighbors are, but that's not the same as knowing them.

I have to spy on the neighborhood from my bedroom window or from the tree stump out in the yard. From there, I can see our neighbors and all their different colors. Our cul-de-sac has families from four different countries: Mexico, India, Iran, and Vietnam. And Dad said Mr. Stanley married a Russian woman last Christmas. I'd love to know how he gets that kind of information, since he doesn't talk to anyone.

What I've noticed from my window is that people in our neighborhood work hard. Every morning I wake up to the coughing sounds of old trucks and vans headed into their worlds. It's not hard to guess at what they do all day. For example, if you need some kind of service, you don't need to call 411. Just look outside your window for the company you want and the number will be painted on the side of a truck or van in big block letters.

JENNINGS PLUMBING

NGUYEN'S PAINTERS

BOB'S POOL SERVICE

Once, when I was sick and stayed home from school, I watched the neighborhood from my window. What I saw was that after all the neighbors leave for work, it's so quiet you could have the whole block to yourself for a few minutes before the school buses appear. Then you will see kids on bikes and on foot head in the same direction. They look like sleepy robots with backpacks.

If the wind picks up, you can hear church-bell chimes swinging from Mrs. Dupree's oak trees. This sound is how I decide if I need to wear a jacket or not. On Mondays you will hear the trash trucks *beepbeepbeep* through the alleys. In the afternoon, if you are superquiet, you can pick up the stop-and-go sound of the postman's truck, which comes to our cul-de-sac around three.

Then in the late afternoon, I noticed that the neighborhood reverses. The school buses come down the streets in the opposite direction, and the schoolkids are the same, maybe with heavier backpacks. The service trucks rumble in from wherever they've been and park back on the street in front of their houses, the men stopping to check the mail. And soon you can smell food cooking on the backyard grills or the stoves, exotic scents that make my mouth water just thinking about them.

While the suppers are cooking, the little kids ride bikes or play hopscotch until their moms call them in with the kinds of accents you've never heard in your life. When the sun fades, the noise of sprinklers and cicadas takes over.

So I guess there's still something left to learn in Garland, after all. It's the fourth Texas town I've called home. Dr. Madrigal would be happy to know this is information I have shared with Lisa.

If you want to know, I have a diary for each city. Four different ones, each a different color. I started out in Galveston (blue), then moved to Waco (yellow), then Tyler (red), and now here I am with a light brown diary in the Land of Gar, which is what Lisa calls this town.

For sheer prettiness, I liked living down in Galveston

by the ocean the best. There was always sand on our kitchen floor, and the windows could stay open almost all year. After work, Dad and I would go for walks next to the gray-green ocean and collect shells. But too many people knew us there, so we had to move. Dad said it made him uncomfortable to even go to the store, which I completely understand.

Right before we left our last house in Tyler, a woman in a low-cut tank top with giant boobs recognized my dad at the Tom Thumb. (Dad later described her boobs as *pendulous*, which is a word I'd like to use more often.)

pendulous *adj*.: hanging down loosely; swinging freely

We'd been searching for ripe peaches, smelling them and finding the best ones, when this woman came up and stared at him like she'd never seen a man. Her eyes traveled all over him, up and down, side to side. There is an ugly way people look when they are judging you. Head turned slightly sideways and nose crinkled like a rotten-food smell just cruised under their nostrils. Giant Boob Lady had that look. If you look in the mirror when you are judging someone, you will never do it again. It is not a pretty sight.

"I'm still not sure if you should've gone to jail," she said.

That was the end of our shopping trip. We just left our cart in the produce area and walked out. I tell you, I've been suspicious of women with pendulous boobs ever since.

chapter 6

The sun is setting now and Dad is still asleep on the couch. I turn down the TV volume and put the brown throw over him. It is strange to think that I'm the one behaving like a parent. Two weeks ago, he said, "No, you can't go with Lisa to the R-rated movie. I don't care that *her* mother says it's okay. What is her cell phone number so I can express my concerns?"

And here it is *me* who puts two Tylenol and a glass of water on the coffee table, where there should be, I don't know, an early birthday present.

I eat a cold Pop-Tart for dinner, put on my faded pajamas, and take myself to bed. I try to sleep but can't. My mind is still churning. This day lacked specialness. I was supposed to be playing with my new iPod by now. Dinner was supposed to be at a restaurant. Pop-Tarts are no substitute for cake.

One of Plant's leaves catches the breeze from the AC vent and waves at me.

"If that boy suddenly finds he understands English and tells someone I've never French-kissed a boy, it could be bad," I tell her. She doesn't answer, not even a wave.

I roll over and stare at the ceiling. Sometimes you do strange things and wonder about yourself later while the ceiling fan spins above you. What if I do weird things because I am going to turn out crazy like my mother? Maybe I need to call a hospital and find out what a person needs to do if they notice the signs. They could study my brain. Then I could get a doctor's note that would get me out of the Family Tree Project.

Sarah is excused for mental-health reasons.

For now, I'm going to stay up all night so I can be awake at the exact moment I turn twelve. Happy birthday to me. Please pass the presents.

At least I've given myself a new paperback book, which I'm almost done reading. It turns out that *rake* is a word I can't add to my vocabulary. Not in the way they use it in *The Valiant Rake*, anyway.

rake *n.*: a dissolute man in fashionable society

And of course, as it often happens with me, I had to look up the definition of a word within a definition.

dissolute *adj.*: indifferent to moral restraints; given to immoral or improper conduct

I've racked my brain for anyone I know who fits the description of a rake. I don't know anyone in fashionable society. But I have seen plenty of older girls who walk around with their underwear peeking out from their jeans. Some of them like to take photographs of this and send them to boys. I will have to investigate if a girl can be a rake. It seems so.

Since tomorrow is my actual birthday, people will be expecting me to use different words. I may be able to throw out *dissolute* in conversation.

I hope twelve is different from eleven. But I hope that every year, and things are mostly the same. I did notice this morning that the things in my room seemed to belong to a younger girl. Maybe that is the first difference. I will have to rearrange my stuff, add some more black to my wardrobe to match my pretty, new headband. I'm hoping my dad will take me to the mall or a movie. Maybe I can guilt him into letting me get my ears pierced. *You know, you were supposed to take me to the mall, but then you got drunk....* Ha! Like I would ever be brave enough to say that out loud.

Sometime after midnight, when I'm officially twelve, I tiptoe through the house as if the floor is made of cotton. Dad is asleep, so there's no way I can make a Pop-Tart without waking him. Our toaster could wake the neighbors it's so loud. So I take it plain and cold and run back to my room. Maybe he'll make pancakes later. Or go get doughnuts, like we do on most Sundays.

Quickly, before he wakes up, I get my real diary out and make a list. I think of my birthday as a fresh start the same way people think of January 1 as a new beginning. My grandmother does this at the beginning of the year. This year, her New Year's goals included trying out an easier hairdo, joining a book club, and growing tomatoes.

I write goals such as improving my posture and my ability to apply green or blue eye shadow. I'd like to know more about Jehovah's Witnesses and why they make my dad ignore the doorbell. What have they witnessed, and why wouldn't you want to know this?

Today, I write my list of new goals in my diary:

- French-kiss a boy.
- Add more variety to my life.
- Get ears pierced.
- Learn a little español.
- Watch for signs of going crazy (ha-ha).

I wish I had my old birthday lists right now. I could go dig them out of my box and read about my old self. I've made my lists since my eighth birthday. My eighth birthday sucked. *Sucked* is a trouble word as huge as Texas, so I don't say it in front of Dad, who is a general know-it-all when it comes to good grammar, since he is a professor. But sometimes you have to use the word that fits, even if you use it only in your mind.

I won't even tell you how bad that birthday was. Let's just say that if I wanted to write an article called "10 Tips for a Horrible Party" I could do it, no problem.

1. Eat cold pizza at Chuck E. Cheese.
2. Come home.
3. Have Dad watch *The Good, the Bad and the Ugly* for the one-millionth time.
4. Give Dad a drink.
5. Give daughter a dollhouse suitable for a five-year-old.
6. Open card from crazy mother.
7. Quiz Dad about crazy mother.
8. Help clean up Dad's "accidentally" spilled drink.
9. Eat cake in silence.
10. Read a book until you fall asleep.

Like I said, sometimes using the exact right word is a must, trouble or not. Is there a better adjective than *sucked* to describe that day? I don't think so.

chapter 7

It's been two weeks since the lousy birthday weekend. It's finally the last lousy day of sixth grade, but is that stopping our English teacher, Mr. Wistler, from trying to stuff one last thing into our brains? No. It is hopeless. Everyone ignores his voice.

I am restless at my desk, wishing I could just slide through the window glass and get started on my flip-flop tan line. Not that my summer is going to be so spectacular. A dull summer is still Problem 1. Same old Houston with the grandparents. Same boring life. Same. Same. Same.

Here are the ingredients of a typical boring Sarah Nelson summer:

- Drive straight to Houston. Do not stop for anything interesting, like World's Largest Boot, Exit E, or Peanut Buster Parfait at Dairy Queen.
- Arrive at grandparents' house and immediately check the Weather Channel.
- Observe Grandma standing at kitchen window for *hours* trying to match blue and black socks.
- Go to Mayor's Meeting downtown because free dinner will be served and wouldn't it be fun to hear a public official speak? (Answer: No.)
- *Finally* arrive at fun day, where Grandma pulls out sewing kit and together we make a stuffed animal such as a red camel with black fringe and she tells me how pretty I am. (Why can't we fast-forward to this part of the summer?)
- Conclude summer with embarrassing shopping trip to mall with Grandma, who buys me little-girl dresses I will never wear, unless there is an awful-dress contest, which I would win, no problem.

That is all I have to look forward to. That and starting my investigation into Problem 2: the dreaded seventh-grade Family Tree Project.

In the meantime, Mr. Wistler keeps talking in that way adults do when they think they are doing you a favor by sharing their intelligence. It's like their own voice is a favorite song. Mr. Wistler goes on and on about "our texting generation," how we know how to think only with our thumbs, how technology is giving way to a condensed language our grandmothers wouldn't recognize, devoid of vowels.

"Would you write this way when you're in front of a computer?" he wants to know. "Or dare I say, have an actual pencil and paper in your hands?"

I inspect my toes, deciding which color I should paint them next, purple or light pink. I like purple better, but it shows all your mistakes if you color outside the lines of your nails, which I sometimes do.

Then Mr. Wistler writes on the blackboard:

Tht wus 2GTBT. OMG! NE1 can c she shrd WTMI ROTFL!!!!!!! GOT 2 GO MOS BCNU

And of course, seeing this written in chalk by a teacher is hilarious, so we have to laugh a tiny bit.

"So I challenge you to write letters to someone, any-one, all summer long. Write with actual *words* and *vowels*. Write a story. Write a book of poetry. Anything. It just has to include correctly spelled words. The way they spell them in the dictionary!"

Ha! I already know how to do that, Mr. W.

"Now before you start saying, 'OMG, Mr. Wistler, are you serious,' just hear me out. I can't give you a grade, because I won't be your teacher next year. So I am offering a reward. A prize!

"Anyone who shows me evidence of actual consistent writing at the beginning of next school year will receive an iPod Nano."

He holds up a shiny plastic case with a green iPod inside. It's possibility wrapped in plastic. I want it.

Someone in the class says the idea is stupid. *Good*, I think. One less person to compete with.

"It's stupid," Mr. Wistler says. "I wonder how you'd text your thoughts. Could you write a complete sentence? Or, is there an acronym for it?"

"Uncool," says Dale Baker. "That's what we'd say."

"Interesting," says Mr. Wistler. "Well, you see, we have a problem. I love to read, and I'm standing in a room full of the next generation of writers. Will I need a special English-to-text dictionary to figure out what your story is about?

"I want you to try this. You write texts to your friends and don't even blink. I'm asking you to write letters, adding in events, things you noticed, how the change of season makes you feel, the scent of flowers. Imagine living in India with a monkey. Be happy just for lemonade on a hot day. Pretend you are a stranger in your own house and

37

you just noticed a crack in the ceiling. Could it be a door to an unknown room? Write letters to someone you see across a restaurant. Maybe a famous person, dead or alive.

"Or even letters to your favorite characters in books or movies. Ask them questions about their life. Their choices. What if Harry Potter came to Texas? Tell him why you like him so much. Write about why he is interesting to *you*. Pretend you will meet him, or any other character, at the end of the summer. Let your mind be curious and blissfully acronym-free."

I look around the room. You can just tell that *every* person in here is now going to write to Harry Potter.

Mr. Wistler says, "And if you don't know anyone, you can write to me. Just be warned, I might write you back!"

"Do we have to do this?" Jimmy Leighton asks.

If you want to know, Jimmy Leighton is the one boy in the entire school who I wish noticed me.

By the way, he's not really in a relationship with Emma Rodriguez. She was just writing fiction on her Facebook page, probably wishing it were so. I don't blame her. Jimmy has the yellowest blond hair and is probably the best-dressed guy in the school.

When I see him, my mind pushes everyone else to the background and pictures him walking in slow motion. That is how nice he is to look at. He had his own Facebook page, and I used to go stare at him there because I could do it in private. But a lot of kids wrote stupid stuff, like he was gay, just because he wore a vest one day, so he took the page down. Seriously, I wish Lucas McCain could come to our school and talk sense to people.

Mr. Wistler tries to explain what he wants to Jimmy Leighton, but I am thinking, *Oh, you còuld write to me, Jimmy. Write to me! I like vests!*

"Mr. Leighton, I cannot make you do this, but I hope you will try."

Mr. Wistler paces the floor now, his hands deep in his pockets. The only time I ever remember him being this agitated was when we read *The Giver*. He then lifts up a big box and starts tossing out composition books to all of us.

"Now, open this book and begin. Write your first sentences of an actual letter or story, and show it to me on the way out the door so I will know I am not just talking to myself, PLZ."

There are so many groans from the class you can't even count them. "I don't know what to write," they all say again. "I can't think of anything, Mr. Wistler. You're killing me." "Mr. Wistler, you're such a buzzkill."

And then Mr. Wistler says, "Most people don't know what they truly think until they write it down. Don't you want to know what you *truly* think?"

The composition book he tossed on my desk is green,

which I take as a sign I am going to win the iPod. I can hear the music. This is easy. I already write more than I talk. I stare at the blank page. The pale blue lines scream to be filled. I bite the eraser on my pencil, wondering what in the world it would be like to live in India with a monkey who drinks lemonade while a tornado passes overhead. There is a giant crack in the ceiling of our hallway at home, and it leads to the attic and all sorts of spiders. There is a good story hiding up there.

Before you can say *summer*, I start writing. And what Mr. Wistler said is true. I didn't know I had this thought.

Dear Mary,
I have a question for you. Does someone remind you it's my birthday, or do you know the date by heart because I don't think you do? And also I'm curious how you spend your own birthday. Do they have cake where you live?

Writing *Dear Mary* was smart, so no one will know what I am talking about. In crime movies, this is called hiding something in plain sight. The problem is, my body didn't want my brain to think this thought, because my neck goes hot and red. I look up from my composition book. Mr. Wistler is smiling. At me. Does he know my secret? I suppose it's possible. Or part of it. Today, however, I might have blown my whole cover, as they also say in crime movies.

I tear the page out, fold it in half, and stuff it in the back of the composition book. *Hurry up,* I say to myself. *Write something else!*

My hand moves as fast as I can make it go.

Dear Atticus Finch,

I am writing to you for a class assignment given to me by the greatest English teacher ever, Mr. G. Wistler. He had the idea that we should choose a character to write to. I can't say for certain, but I think I'm the only one writing to you. That is good for me. Most of my classmates are writing to Harry Potter and Lucy Moon. Maybe you've met them at the library. When I was little, I used to think that when the library closed, all the characters came out of the books.

Anyway, I have to admit I didn't read about you first. You probably know that a movie has been made from the book about you. I watched you late one night when my father was watching the movie *To Kill a Mockingbird*. He said it was a good story. Then he fell asleep halfway through, but I kept watching. This was about a year ago. There were so many things to like about the story. Then I found out we had a paperback copy of the book in the house. I read it in four days.

Mr. Wistler said we should tell you what we thought was the most interesting thing about the character we chose. He said we should think of one or two questions we'd ask you if we had the chance to sit with you at the breakfast table and talk. The biggest question that comes into my head is, Why did you decide to represent Tom Robinson? I know you said in the book that it was the right thing to do. People don't always do the right thing, though. The way I know something is the right thing to do is if I write down all my choices and then circle the one that is the hardest. The hardest is almost always the right thing to do. But it is the one that can get you in trouble, too. I wonder if you did the same thing. I would like to ask you, Did you sit on your front porch and list all your choices about representing Tom Robinson? Did you know ahead of time that people would call you names and make fun of you? To me, you made the right choice. That is why you are so compelling to me. Also, I like the way you talk to your children, Scout and Jem. I would like to have breakfast with all of you.

Sincerely,
Sarah Nelson

The bell rings. Only a few kids let Mr. Wistler look at their first sentence. There will be a pile of empty composition books in the hallway trash can, you can bet.

Mr. Wistler reads my letter and hands the composition book back to me like it is something fragile. "Hmmm," he says. "Now this is an interesting letter, especially the part about the great English teacher. I hope you'll keep writing, Sarah. I like how you write."

"Thank you." I take the book, head toward the door.

"Hey, Sarah," he says. I turn back and see him holding the iPod. He tosses it in the air, and I miraculously catch it. I've never caught a ball or anything in my life.

"Don't tell anyone," he says with a wink.

I say thank you, but it comes out like a whisper.

"Now go have the best summer of your life," he says.

Ha! That's the hardest assignment he could give me. At least now, my boring summer can have its own sound track.

I walk into the hallway, feeling weird. In the first trash bin, I spot a couple of composition books. I hope no one is looking, and I grab them, opening the first one.

DEAR HARRY POTTER,

I stuff them into my backpack along with the iPod.
I pack up my locker, gathering mostly junk and bits of

paper, down to the last piece of gum. No evidence left behind. I consider the composition book again and pray I don't die on the way home where some ambulance worker would find the *Dear Mary* letter hidden there. *At least let me get home, God, so I can tear it up into a million pieces.*

chapter 8

I have to be careful with Lisa. You could say she is my best friend, but when you hardly have any friends, *best* is relative. She is a friend and she is there, and if I didn't have *any* girlfriends, I would stand out like a blue sunflower. She says she can tell things about a girl by the way her neck is tilted.

So when she comes up to me and asks, "What's up with you? You're blushing. OMG, did you get a note from a boy?" I have to straighten out my neck and say, "No way."

Lisa's smile is accessorized by supershiny pink lip gloss today, her hair pulled away from her face by a neat plaid headband. I've never seen her unhappy. I like that about her. If Lisa were a color, she would be yellow.

Also, she gave me a pair of earrings for my birthday.

Earrings. For pierced ears.

She is such a teaser.

She said, "Now he'll have to let you get them pierced."

"You're delusional."

"Just try."

What she doesn't know about my dad could fill a book. A book Lisa would never read.

"Let's go, let's go," she says in the fast and breathless way she has. Another thing about Lisa is she usually wants to be at the next place, not where she actually is.

So we sprint out of the school, talking fast about her fun plans to go away to camp and would I write her and "don't forget our pact to have French-kissed a boy by the end of the summer, text me as soon as it happens." She is set on this kind of kiss for some reason, as if it will change her life. She thinks it will show on the outside after it happens, make her seem older, hold her head differently.

I'm not so sure this is so, and even if it is, why would you want the world to know your business? Personally, I would rather have a boy notice the book I was reading and tell me he liked it, too. That seems like a better sign of caring about someone than a kiss some French guy invented.

Mr. Wistler, my new favorite person on the planet, says giving characters a lot of experiences makes them interesting. What I think is, this must be so in real life, too, so I'm going to try to add variety to myself this summer, and a French kiss would sure be different, which is the reason it's on my list. It will be hard to do. How I will find someone to kiss while I'm banished to my grandparents' house for the entire summer, I have no idea. They don't even have a lawn boy.

Lisa meets her mother at the car line, and I head for the bus line.

It's a party on wheels inside the bus today. Well, it's the last day, after all. And the last bus ride, which if I were a person who says "Thank God!" all the time, I would say "Thank God this is the last day I have to ride a bus!" I would rather walk the whole way home, but no, that will never happen, because of my dad and his "concerns about my safety." He should ride on the bus, and then he would have real concerns about my safety.

For example, people usually smell bad and are not nice to new kids, especially if you are a lowly sixth grader. When you're a sixth grader, kids don't have to have any good reason to bother you other than your age. The good thing about being me is I've learned how to find the Darts on the bus before they get me. *Darts* is a private word I made up.

Darts *n.*: kids who find a person's weakness and go out of their way to be mean

I can use this word and insult them without them knowing. Besides, it fits. I picture their mean words flying through the air and stabbing the person they're hurled at. Darts are not hard to pick out. They like to have an audience, and they come in sets of two or three. They have whatever is the New Thing before anyone else. They talk loudly. They think they know everything. And they don't bring their lunch, which makes me want to ask, *Where is your mother?* But I don't. I stay invisible like always.

Especially today.

There are two Darts on my bus: Mark Medina and Daryl Land. They would love to steal my iPod or make fun of my letter to Atticus or both if they knew about them. It is a good thing these are hidden in the super-secret compartment of my backpack. Daryl is the leader of a whole group of Darts. He has a green camo backpack, and his shoes don't have laces, which I guess he thinks is cool. I think it's kind of dorky, but I would never say this out loud.

At the beginning of the year, there was a new kid named Russell. I could have told Russell his clarinet case with a Boy Scout sticker on it was going to get him pinged with darts, but I didn't say anything. Daryl Land called him a doofus and a wuss. Russell stood there for a moment and then pushed his way past, but Daryl shoved him right into a seat and threw his case down. Russell tried to talk, but whatever he was thinking took about an hour to say because he stuttered. This was bad for him because Daryl drowned him in insults.

It got so bad I got mad at Russell for not defending himself, for not just finding another way to go home, another ride. But I guess the difference between me and Russell is, I have a garage full of packing boxes ready to fill if we need to leave. Plus, I am a coward. I see Russell getting hurt and I do nothing because I'd rather it be him than me.

Today, Russell isn't on the bus. You have to wonder if Russell loves summer and being off a bus more than anything in the world.

I live two blocks from where the school bus lets me off. I want to take off my sandals and walk on the newly cut grass, feel the start of summer under my feet, maybe follow the warm tar lines in the middle of the street. Plus, this will be the last time I will get to be completely alone for a while. I am tired of fighting with my dad about being sent away all summer. It is no use.

This is what happened last night.

At dinner, he'd said, "We need to start making our summer plans." He didn't look at me when he said it. He'd just stared at the menu. We'd gone out to eat because somebody forgot to go to the grocery store and no one wanted a can of soup.

"I guess so," I said, trying hard to think how I could convince him I was old enough to stay at home. Since my dad is a professor, he is trained to find the holes in arguments. You have to be careful, say short sentences that don't give too much information.

"Gramps is looking forward to taking you fishing," he said. "And there are some new exhibits coming to the museums this year. Maybe a trip to the boardwalk in Kemah." He closed his menu and looked across at me, eyebrows raised as if he'd asked a question. Sure, Gramps will sometimes take me along when he goes fishing with his friends. I bring a book. And museums? People have different ideas about what's fun.

"I told you," I said. "I don't want to go. And you said we would discuss it."

"Sarah, you know I have to work."

"And I have to live!"

"Don't be so dramatic."

"You have to let me stretch or I will never learn anything. I'm twelve."

"Barely."

"What did you do at twelve?" I asked, but I already know a few facts. He got to go to all kinds of Boy Scout camps away from home and ride his bike without a helmet.

"I would worry about you being home alone all day," he said. "I can't help it."

If Dad looked up *worrier* in *my* dictionary, he might change his ways.

worrier *n.*: a person who thinks about unfortunate things that might happen (see also: **Tom Nelson**)

Well, I could have reminded him about his being drunk and leaving me all alone and never making it to the mall and say, *well, did you worry then?* But no, I didn't.

I just said, "I *really* don't want to go this summer."

He paid the check and we left.

When we got home, I walked in first and stayed silent as he called after me. "Sarah. Sarah, come on! It's because I love you."

"Whatever, Dad," I said, trying to control my quivering voice. It was no use. I sounded shaky.

"I'm not saying you aren't a responsible girl, Sarah," he started.

"But you *are* saying that."

I stomped down the hallway, slammed the door, and waited for him to stand on the other side. It was a long time before he spoke.

"Kiddo, I'll try to think of something, okay? I'll try to think of some other options for the summer, okay?"

I said nothing, let him wait.

"And I'll make it up to you about the mall. We'll go when Grandma gets here."

"Yeah, if you don't get drunk," I'd said.

I'd thought it would feel good to throw his mistake in his face. It didn't. It made me feel like a stupid Dart.

chapter 9

Since it's the last day of school, I take my time walking home from the bus, circle the block a few times, pretend I live on another street. No more school or school buses or Darts for three whole months. But then, I don't want to get home fast, either.

If there were someplace to exist between school and home, wouldn't I like to live there? Yes, I would.

I pass the house with the potted plant displayed on the stump. I feel it staring at me, calling for help. I take a few more steps, and then I can't take it anymore. I run back, rescue it from the stump, and gently place it on their porch, where it's supposed to be — doesn't everybody know that? Did anyone see me? The neighbors will think I'm crazy, but I don't care.

I walk quickly from the crime scene and turn onto Yale Court. I allow myself the luxury of a treasure hunt and pick up a heart-shaped rock—these are easier to spot than you might imagine. Then a golf ball from Mr. Gustafson's front yard. I have two at home that I put little faces on with a black marker. One is a happy face, one is sad. I find it useful to put these on my father's bathroom counter so he'll know my mood.

This morning I'd put them both on his shaving towel. I might have to create a new golf ball with a half-happy, half-sad face on it because lately I feel divided all the time. Half of me fighting to go north, the other half south. Plant suggested this is a sure sign of crazy and to be on the lookout for new voices.

I walk around the whole cul-de-sac, kicking a rock. I check the mail.

There it is.

Somehow I knew it would be there. Now here's one thing you need to know about my mother: She sends me cards twice a year, for my birthday and for Christmas. I don't get anything else from her the rest of the year. This is the way it's always been.

It gives me a tiny bit of fear. I have to remind myself it's just a card. But she has touched this piece of paper, and that makes it a rare thing. It's like we've both been to the same place, just at different times. Like I was going into a building and she was coming out.

At first, I pretend I don't care about her card and read the other mail first. Then, I go say hi to Plant and twist her pot around so she can sun her backside. I check phone messages and send a text to Lisa.

Write me from camp!

Mr. Wistler would be happy that I wrote the text in a complete sentence.

All of this eats up about five minutes.

The envelope stares at me.

It has her loopy handwriting and a Texas Department of Criminal Justice stamp on the outside.

I put my fingers over the ink writing bearing my name.

Sarah Nelson

I let my finger run under the envelope flap and feel a satisfying lift as the paper peels up. I pull out a card and flip it onto its front. I smell the card, hold it up to the light to see if there's a hidden message written in invisible ink. I've read that crazy people sometimes do things like that. But there's nothing like that. Just a picture of a black Labrador dog staring back at me. His head is tilted as if someone just asked him to do Algebra and he's thinking, *Are you kidding?*

I open the card.

Have a Doggone Happy Birthday.

And then, in her handwriting:

Happy Birthday, Sarah. How are you doing? Twelve is such a wonderful age. Please send me pictures of your new self.

Love, ~~Jane~~ Your Mother

Okay, this isn't nice, but right off, there are two mistakes in this card:

1. She first signed the card *Jane*.
2. She thinks I have a new self.

I have to wonder if somebody at her hospital reminded her not to sign her name to her own daughter's birthday card. And what does she know about my new self? She knows nothing about me.

Still, I go into my bathroom to see if a new self stares back. I run my hand through my hair. Push it back behind my ears so maybe it will look put up. Pucker my lips and twist my shoulders to the side, supermodel-style. I don't know; maybe there is a small change, but it's just the difference between six and six-o-five — the same plain me, only five minutes older.

Maybe she just wrote the word for no reason and I'm

getting all excited over nothing. Analysis is paralysis, Gramps always says when we are all trying to decide on a place to eat and none of us can make up our minds. I'm thinking about this too much. I set the card aside, tell myself she wants a picture of me, nothing more. The worst part of the whole "crazy mother" issue is, there is no one I can talk to about this card.

"What do you think, Simon?" I say to my reflection. "Does twelve look different to you? Do I look different from where you are?"

Right away, I feel lonely for Simon, so I erase my thoughts about him, think about someone new.

My aunt Mariah?

I could call her and ask her what she thinks. She is another person our family doesn't like to talk about, probably because she is my mother's half sister. I wish we were closer, but we are not. When I think of her, I picture her quoting the Bible and grabbing both of my hands together when she greets me. My grandmother doesn't like this much at all. Aunt Mariah is a touchy person, decorated with jewelry and color. If people were colors, my grandmother would be beige and Aunt Mariah a rainbow. Ha!

I close my eyes and picture her hands on my face. Yes, I could talk to her about this card. I will have to write it on my list, ask my dad for her phone number. I don't know when I talked to her last.

Simon comes to my mind again, and I have to tell him to please go away now.

When we were in Galveston, my aunt and I had a lot of long walks on the beach. She would put her face close to mine, and I could smell the mint leaf she liked to chew. She'd say the most amazing things, which made you wish you had a pencil and paper attached to your shirt. You'd want to catch all her phrases.

"There are people just waiting to love you, people God has put along the path of life like signposts down a highway. Go This Way. Turn Here and Love This Person. Help: 10 Miles. Most do not stop to read them, Sarah girl."

One thing I remember for sure is this: She said if I love someone else when I most need to feel loved, well, then love will rain over me until I am soaked.

It is at this moment I realize I am crying.

Tears flow, and I hug the card to my chest. I slide down onto the yellow bathroom floor and lie on my side, and I see one of my barrettes under the cabinet. I feel split in two. I ache to know more about my mother, while at the same time, I wish she'd never send me any cards at all. Feeling two things at once must be one of the first signs of going crazy.

After a few minutes, I hear the sound of our garage door opening. It rattles and screeches like something is killing it.

I get up from the floor and straighten myself out. My cheeks are red and splotchy, so I splash water on my face and then run into my room, close the door, and sit next to Plant. Her birthday is in September, so she will have to wait for something special. I read her my birthday card.

"I wonder if she was signing a bunch of autographs and they put this card in front of her," I say. "She thought it was just another signature for a fan."

I've read on the Internet about people who want to write to my mother. From what I can tell, there are some men who have a crush on her, some women who want to hurt her, and some people who want to study her. It is strange to think how some people know more about her than I do. It is so unfair.

chapter 10

I look out the window and see doom on wheels.

The giant beige town car turns into our driveway. It means boredom. It means that Dad didn't think of any other options for the summer.

"Hello!" Gramps shouts. He is first to catch me as I walk to the kitchen. He squeezes my shoulder. I was hoping I could sneak a quick snack, hide in my room, and open my iPod.

My grandmother hugs me.

"Would you like some lemonade?" she wants to know. "I brought some with me."

My dad pats my back.

Squeeze. Hug. Pat.

The same thing every time I see them together. At least they can't see I've been crying. Or they don't notice.

"How was the last day of school?" Gramps asks.

"Did you learn anything new today?" Grandma asks.

My skin is electric with irritation. Can't I get a minute alone? I don't want Lisa to go to camp. I wish I didn't have a stupid Labrador wishing me a doggone happy birthday, asking me about my "new" self. And I can't stand the idea of going to Houston, where fun goes to die. I am a mix of angry and sad. No investigator could handle all the questions bubbling up, no matter how smart he is.

"Be right back," I say.

No, I won't. I'm going to be gone until you make me come out.

Maybe this is another sign of going crazy, but I do my best writing in my closet, which is where I go to write another letter.

Dear Atticus,
Here I am, writing to you again. Don't ask me why, but I just felt like I needed to. Also, I have this new iPod (you don't know what that is, but trust me, it's cool) and three new composition books, and I feel like I should fill them up. I wasn't sure how to begin this letter. I thought of writing *Dear Mr. Finch*, out of respect. I know your own kids called you by your first name instead of calling you Dad or Father. I wondered about this the first time I read the

book in which you appear. My dad (Tom Nelson) told me it was because you were trying to teach Scout and Jem how to respect elders. I suppose that might have been true in your time, but I know a girl in my class who calls her mother Lori when she won't answer to Mom. We have discovered that this gets an adult's attention if they are ignoring you and talking on the phone. This is how she says it. "Excuse me, *Loreeee*." I don't think that's how your kids mean it when they call you Atticus. You seem to pay attention to them. Plus, it seems that Harper Lee, the author, liked to name the pets in her story with full names. I know because I circled them in my paperback. There's that mad dog named Tim Johnson and the cat named Rose Aylmer and the sheriff's dog, Ann Taylor. I never thought to give a pet two names. Maybe in Alabama this is how things are done.

As you know, my English teacher, Mr. Wistler, told our class to write to our favorite character. You are mine. I have others who I considered, like Boo Radley. But for many reasons, people who read this letter might roll their eyes and say, "I knew that girl would write to the oddest character and not someone normal." So I will keep my questions for Boo to myself. Also, I thought a long time about writing to Scout. That is true. The thing is, I would like to be Scout, because she is tough sometimes but can still be like a girl. Sometimes I think about the things she might do and wonder if I would make the same choices. But I realized that if I wrote to Scout, all my words would add up to this: Atticus, I wish you were my father. You are the only one I could picture reading my letter and not laughing at me. I imagine you sitting on your porch, holding this paper, and reading the whole letter before you even respond. Is that strange? Maybe it is, but I'd be lying if I said I'd never had an imaginary conversation before. I am twelve years old, just so you know.

If you could really talk back to me, I would like to ask, is it hard to be a parent without a wife? For you, it doesn't seem too hard, maybe because by the time your story is told, your kids are school-age and you have a nice maid, Calpurnia. I love that name. If I ever have a cat, I will name her Calpurnia. Maybe Finch as her last name. Calpurnia Finch.

I would also like to know how it is you turned out so well with good manners. How did you come to be so patient and kind? What I think I like best about you is that you would be the same most every day if you were my father. If you said you were going to bring spaghetti home for dinner, you would. If you said you were going to teach me how to play a card game, you would explain the rules in a soft, even voice. And I'm sure you would think it would be all right for me to stay home during the summertime while you are at work. How did you get to be so reliable? Was it from your own parents? You see, if you get to know me, you will realize that I think about this kind of thing a lot. I wonder, for example, how much of my mother is inside me and how much is my father. So do you think you are more like one than the other? If you say yes, there is hope for me. I will save that story for another letter. As many people like to say, that would be TMI, or too much information.

Sincerely,
Sarah Nelson

chapter 11

My grandmother knocks on the door to my bedroom. Quick like a shot, I am out of my closet.

"Sarah, where would you like to go for dinner?"

"Be out in a minute."

Nope. Still not coming out. I'm going to climb out the window and run away. You will have to find dinner on your own.

She says, "Looking forward to talking about summer plans with you. Maybe we'll go to Chuck E. Cheese!"

"Okay," I say.

It's all the enthusiasm I can muster.

Chuck E. Cheese and I don't get along.

The last time I was there, if you'll remember, was the year of the sucky birthday party and the little-girl dollhouse and the spilled drink, which was all Jim Beam then. This was before Jim Beam met Dr Pepper.

I said I wasn't going to talk about it, but here I am with a card from Jane, aka my mother. This birthday is starting to feel like that one.

At least my mother remembered. I have nothing from Dad.

When I turned eight, he gave me two stuffed animals, a charm-locket necklace, a stack of books, a play makeup kit, pink leopard-print slippers, a water bottle with my initials on it, a yellow diary, and the little-girl dollhouse.

It was pink, of course.

Each room of the dollhouse had a little light on the ceiling, and you could turn each one of them on and off. There were even pictures on the walls of happy faces, which I suppose were meant to be the family members of the dolls.

My mother's birthday card was on the floor next to me.

"Why do I only get a card?" I asked. "Why don't I get more from her?"

"I don't know, Sarah," he said, his face still glued to the TV.

"Maybe because you move so much, she didn't get our new address."

"I gave it to her. She knows."

"Can we call her right now and ask? Maybe there's something else."

"I'll ask next time, but I don't think there's anything else."

"Do you think her brain will ever get well?"

"I don't know."

"I wonder what she was like when she was eight."

"That was about when her own mother died. She moved to her father's house in South Texas."

"So we are alike?"

"Well, yes. Maybe."

"I want to paint her a picture. What does she like?"

"I don't know. She'll like whatever you draw."

"You just don't want to tell me."

"Sarah, I really don't…"

His thick glass slipped from his fingers and made a loud crash against the tile floor. Glass and ice everywhere. I don't know if it was dropped or thrown.

I sat back in my birthday-paper nest and tried to be an invisible pink thing.

"Sorry, kiddo. I don't know how that slipped…." And then he couldn't finish his sentence.

He was trying not to cry.

A gunfight played out on the TV. In a strange way, it was comforting. The good guys were winning.

"I'm sorry I made you upset."

"You don't make me upset, Sarah," he said. "You are my curious girl."

I helped him clean up the glass and the ice cubes. I smelled it just to see what Jim Beam was all about. It reminded me of cough syrup.

That day, I tried to stop being a curious girl in public. I became curious in private. I went through his things when he wasn't home or was sleeping.

That's when I saw the shoe box.

It was on the top shelf, pushed to the back corner of his closet. When I opened it, I discovered what detectives might call an item of interest.

Dear Jane,

I know we talk on the phone some and in e-mails, but I never hear you laugh. I wish I knew what made you laugh. What does make you laugh? Oh, what a horrible letter this is. Look how many times I've written the word 'laugh'? Well, I don't mind admitting it HERE because no one ever reads all my unsent letters—but I've been drinking. Yes, it's true. Mother has done her best to rehabilitate me, and mostly it has worked. Well, really, it is Sarah I do it for. But sometimes, it's the only way I can sleep. I am weak. I am a weak, weak man.

The letter ended, with no closing, no "Love, Tom" or anything. Maybe he had fallen asleep.

You see, this is what happens when you get only a couple of cards a year from a person you don't understand. Someone ends up spilling a drink or crying or both, and you get nowhere.

chapter 12

I wonder if they would notice if I vanished.

"Where did she go?"

"I don't know."

"Let's have another drink."

Since I can't disappear completely, I push the window screen out, climb outside, and replace the screen like a criminal. I know how to cover my tracks. Then I'm up on the dead tree stump in our front yard. This stump is only about three feet high, but at least I am off the ground. You wouldn't think things look that different from this height, but they do. I would love to be this tall in real life. It would give me an edge to see things coming before they got close.

The best I can hope for is to wait things out until that last good week in Houston. I will admire my grandmother's earrings, talk her into letting me get my ears pierced just as she is beginning to like me again.

I look back at our house. My grandmother's nose is up to the window glass. I look away but can still feel her stare. I would bet ten dollars they are having the same conversation they had the last time my grandparents came to Garland.

"That dead tree stump is an eyesore, Tom. Can't you get rid of it?"

"The owners have to take care of it. Plus, she likes standing up there."

"You mean she's done this sort of thing before?"

"What's the big deal?"

"It's odd."

I would hate it if they took down my stump.

Still, I try to imagine what I look like to my grandmother. Standing on a tree stump for no reason is definitely in her category of "things frowned upon." Things frowned upon is big with my grandmother.

Maybe I should ask them to take a picture someday to see if I look like a total dork. Even if I do, I'm trying hard not to care. I've been twelve for about ten minutes, but I know this: I am different from the rest of this family, and it makes them nervous. Maybe they are waiting for signs of crazy, too.

I leap from the stump and swing back through the door. I make an extra effort to say something nice to my grandmother to get things rolling my way. This should improve my chances for pierced ears. I look down at what I'm wearing.

"Well, I can't go someplace nice in *this*." I note the pleased look on her face. She's thinking, *It's as if Sarah read my mind!* "I'll go put on something else."

I feel her smile warm my back as I walk down the hall to my room. Now that I am twelve, I wonder how I should change this room. The truth is that it never went with my eleven-year-old self, either. It's still a sight of pure embarrassment to me, which is why I haven't had any friends over except Lisa, and then all she does is say, "Let's ask your dad to take us to the mall."

If you want to know, my room looks like Pepto-Bismol threw up inside it. Nothing left untouched. Pink walls. Pink throw rug. Nubby pink bedspread. Pink lamp shade. My dad thinks this is what a girl wants. I almost told him how awful it was when he opened the door almost two years ago and introduced me to my new room, but then he handed me my first cell phone.

Also pink.

What could I do?

The closet is the one place inside my weird room most

like me. Small and private. It is some pale white color that changes depending on the time of day and the light from the window. When I sit inside my closet, I imagine I'm watching the girl who used to live here. In my mind, she is a blond, happy girl who reads and makes beaded bracelets with her friends' names on them. She is a girl who likes pink.

I also have a large black box at the back of my closet.

Another girl might think the box is full of junk, but for me, it is full of memories. Every time we move, I have to rethink what's important, what will fit inside this box. Some things have to be thrown out, and the rest I have to keep in my mind. There's a ticket stub to the first real movie my dad took me to, *The Polar Express*. A postcard from my aunt Mariah with a giant picture of the Texas coast on the front. A picture I cut out of a magazine of a beagle puppy, the kind of dog you know you could tell all your secrets to. A bottle cap Gramps gave me, or, really, pretended to take out of my ear. I sometimes keep my fake diary in this box because it is the most obvious place.

And of course, I also have her cards. A small stack tied with a black ribbon.

If this were Dad's closet, I'd stuff all these cards in the holes in the walls. The holes are the exact size of a fist. Last time I checked, there were three.

I look through my clothes and pick out a white shirt

73

and capri pants. I brush my hair back behind my ears, put on my new sparkly headband. My grandma is sure to see my earlobes. They practically scream nakedness.

Dad, Gramps, and Grandma are sitting in the peach-colored, semicircle booth at La Norte Tex Mex with me sandwiched in the center. This is my favorite booth in my favorite restaurant. They have Christmas lights up all year and weird wooden cat, pig, and bird figures on the walls. My grandmother says it's too over-the-top, and I always wonder, *Over the top of what?* It's hard to have a bad time in a place with this many colors. Plus, free chips and salsa as soon as you sit down. You could just eat chips and run out of the place without ever paying, but we never do.

The waitress brings our drinks and takes our orders. Sour-cream enchiladas with double rice and no beans, thank you very much.

"So, Sarah," Dad says. Here it comes. Here comes somebody else's idea of a fun summer for Sarah Nelson. I have to remind myself that Dad is not used to having fun and doesn't care if others despair for happiness, which is my favorite line from *The Valiant Rake*. Someone is often despairing about something in that book.

"Remember Charlotte Reynolds? She's home from college and wants you to call her."

Of course I remember Charlotte.

I *love* Charlotte. She was the first girl to point out that my toenails should always be painted, even in winter. Also, last year she left me a stack of magazines and books as tall as a three-year-old. Magazines I would never ask my father to get for me.

And the books Charlotte gave me were the best kind. Paperbacks with the edges worn smooth and a bunch of pages dog-eared and sections highlighted in yellow. They were all her favorite stories from high school, she said, telling me to read *To Kill a Mockingbird* first, which, of course, I did. It was the second time I'd read it.

The other great thing about Charlotte is she has a brother who delivers pizza. That is a real plus if your dad forgets to buy food. They both live right across the street from us when they're not away at college. When she was home for Christmas, we spent one whole afternoon reading, a box of cold pizza on the coffee table for our eating convenience.

"Yes, I remember Charlotte," I say, wondering why I didn't already know she was home and does she have a different car?

"I talked to her, and she's looking forward to seeing you this summer."

Seeing me where, exactly? Will she be in Houston? "That's nice."

"Charlotte has to study a lot over the summer. She'll

be home a lot," he says. "Well, I asked her if she wouldn't mind you staying at her house during the day. You know, just until I get home from work."

This is unbelievable! I don't have to go to my grandparents' house. I am getting a reprieve, which I've actually seen happen only in the movies.

reprieve *n.*: a respite from impending punishment

I feel my body relax. It's as if I've been holding my breath for a week and someone finally said, *It's okay, you can let it go.*

At home, I let myself daydream about the summer. In a few short days I'd get to hang out with Charlotte, plan my time around what I wanted to do. I am getting ready to write about these new developments in my real diary when Dad knocks on my door.

"So, we're all set, then?"

"Yes," I say.

He hugs me and I let him. I've outgrown the long hugs he likes to give. But how can I refuse him now? I hug him back tighter, and I swear I can feel the corners of his mouth go up. Mine do, too. When he lets go of me, he puts the unhappy-face golf ball in my palm and closes my fingers around it.

"Can I come in?"

Grandma just helps herself on in before we can say anything.

Grandma sits down on my bed and hands me a small purple gift bag.

"Happy birthday," she says. "You look like you could use this, and even if you can't, you can start training."

I pull out a bra. It's pink, of course, and hideous.

"Just as I thought," Grandma says.

Not only does she hold the bra to my chest, but she does it in front of my dad. I am about to despair of ever showing my face to the world again. When I look over at him, I see him staring at my dresser.

When they leave my room, I look at the green composition book sitting there, the envelope from my mother next to it. Why did I leave that out in the open?

After they are gone, I hide everything. The composition book. The envelope. The new pink bra. The next family to rent this house will find all of it in an unusual place and wonder what kind of strange family lived here.

I know I do.

chapter 13

Charlotte's perfection makes our dumpy sofa look extra dumpy.

She sits with her legs crossed at the ankles and her hands in her lap over a white flowing skirt, looking calm and ladylike. There's something flawless and different about Charlotte. Of course, she is twenty and you would hope a person would have achieved perfection by that age. Compared with me, she is store-bought and I'm homemade. Whenever I got nervous in school last year, I would say to myself, "How would Charlotte act now?" and do whatever came to mind, which was usually pretending I didn't care.

This was some of the best advice I have given myself, I can tell you.

"Hi," I say to her.

Charlotte says, "So, I need to go to the grocery store. Want to come?"

See what I mean? I haven't seen her for months, but we are already going shopping like two best friends.

I throw a look to my dad, who says, "Of course. You girls have fun."

"I'll get you some Funyuns."

"The big package, please. I have papers to grade." He winks at me then. Whenever he has a thick chunk of student papers, he always likes to have a bag of chips nearby. He says it actually makes the bad papers read better, but I think this is just an excuse to eat Funyuns.

I skip across the street and slide into Charlotte's car, which is about as low to the ground as a car can be without actually touching the street. She turns up the volume on the radio and rolls down the windows. This is just how I like it.

I watch her in profile as she drives with confidence, the way I will one day soon. Even just seeing one side of her face, you know Charlotte is beautiful. She has the qualities magazines say go into a pretty face. Smooth skin, green eyes, and a great smile set off by pink lip gloss that never gets stuck on her teeth. To me, she is the kind of girl a handsome farmer would spot across a field and want to be his wife just by looking at her. Well, maybe I've seen too many Westerns, but I swear that's how she looks. She also doesn't ask me a ton of questions, which is a real plus.

At a stoplight, she says, "I don't even know where to get Funyuns."

"Sometimes you have to go to the dollar store."

"I'm not going there."

Charlotte is sophisticated. I shouldn't have mentioned the dollar store. I am a dork. I love the dollar store because my allowance doesn't run out and there is always something you'd never think existed on the planet, like a coin purse made out of a sock.

"I have to make two casseroles today, and I need your help."

This is something else I love about Charlotte. She doesn't wonder if I can help. She just assumes I can.

"Who died?" I ask.

"What? Nobody died."

"I thought casseroles were the official food of grieving. Or if something bad happens."

"Turns out they are also the official food of hungry young men. Or at least the one I'm in love with."

Love?

This is news with a capital *N*. I have a million questions because I have not yet fallen in love. As soon as Jimmy Leighton notices me, it should happen right away. But there are things I need to know. Is there a moment where you know someone and it's normal and then he picks up the book you dropped from your backpack and — *boom* — five minutes later you are in love? And when do you know you should start moving in for a kiss like they do in movies? Who is supposed to turn their head so noses don't get smashed?

It's superloud inside my head right now, so I just play it cool and say, "Oh, that's nice."

"Do you like boys yet?" Charlotte asks. "Or are you at the age where you still think boys are smelly and stupid?"

"It depends on their age, I guess," I say. "But most boys I know are plain weird." Except for Jimmy Leighton. He is weird in a good way.

The truth is, I do notice boys, and I am curious about what they think, what their rooms look like, and, of course, the kissing part. I know the basic things about them: They are crazy to see even a piece of a girl's underwear; when they get on the bus, they talk loud; they get in trouble for stupid things, like writing *Visit Pen Island* on the blackboard; and, when they skateboard through my neighborhood, they look fearless. Sometimes I wonder if Simon would be like them. He would be a skateboarder, for sure.

"Well, one day you will learn all about it," she says. "For now, take my word on it. It's extraordinary."

Charlotte is the kind of person who can use the word

extraordinary just like that. Most people save this word to describe a bad storm or a painting at the museum, but no, she can say it in Garland on a hot day. I let the muscles of my mouth form the word without making a sound. I try it on to see if it fits. *Why, these chips are just extraordinary!*

No, that sounds wrong. I'll have to wait for love to talk like her.

"Don't you want to know everything about him?"

"Do *you* know everything about him?" I ask.

"I know a lot of things about him," she says. "The important things."

I want her to write a list of them for me right now. I put my hands under my legs and dig my nails into the seat so I won't say anything stupid.

"He works at Wilson's Western Wear at the mall, and he likes King Ranch casserole, which is our particular mission today. We are going to figure out how to make one."

Well, this is why I love Charlotte. We both know that occupation and favorite foods are important facts to know about a person. I am all of a sudden wondering about Casserole Man and how he must think Charlotte is extraordinary, too, and what this might mean to my blissful, grandparent-free summer. Somewhere during my private thinking, we arrive at the grocery store.

Charlotte is out of the car and three steps ahead of me before I know it. I run to catch up with her, and one of my flip-flops comes off in the parking lot. I feel her eyes scanning me, and I try my best to look natural. I follow her into the store and think about how Charlotte might help me persuade Dad to let me get my ears pierced. They should be pierced before I have a real kiss from a boy.

During the school year, Lisa and I had a boy party. We had to be secretive. If we had said to her mother, "Hey, we want to have a boy party," well, that would have put an end to parties for the rest of our lives. We had three girls and three boys at her house. Her mother made popcorn and ordered pizzas. All of us would stay inside for a while or go and take walks outside. Outside seemed a mile from Lisa's mother. I imagined her thinking, *Oh, those kids are just getting some fresh air, looking at the constellations. They aren't doing anything else.*

But maybe her mother didn't care what we were doing outside. Or maybe her mother had been eleven years old once and remembered what it felt like to never have been kissed. The kissing-pact stuff came up then. Lisa and her brilliant idea.

For a long time, it seemed to me like it's just two parts of the body touching and why should it be any different than knuckles or knees? We stole some of the romance novels Lisa's mother kept under her bed and learned how it could be more, though I had to go to the dictionary and

Google a few times for more explanation. If you believe the paperbacks, a strange feeling makes a person want to kiss another person.

In the romance novels, the person usually gets that kind of feeling when it's raining or when she sees a shirtless guy hiding behind her bedroom curtains. And for some reason Lisa and I could never figure out, the woman isn't afraid of the stranger. If it were me, it would be 911 city.

What's my emergency? There's a stranger in my room! Help!

I don't know much about much, but I do know the black-and-white definition of something leaves out the important fact. The one you feel but can't describe. And someday I'm going to get the courage to ask Lisa's mom about those books.

Lisa invited Renee to our party. Renee is the prettiest of the three of us. She has shampoo-commercial blond hair, the envy of everyone.

Lisa invited Jimmy Leighton to the party. He acted shy and quiet, which is when I started to have a crush on him. David Watters and Steven Ng were there, too, but they are big show-offs. They skateboard all over Garland and like to tell you so. And if you ask me, David is the one who started calling Jimmy gay. Here are my thoughts on him: Whatever!

But Steven Ng is one of the cutest boys you will ever see. His hair is perfect, and when he smiles, his whole face shows happiness.

So there we were at this party, the boys hogging the pizza and the girls sitting together watching *The Unborn*. I watched to see if Jimmy Leighton would flinch during the scary parts. He didn't. After, we all went outside, and, wouldn't you know it, Steven and David got on their skateboards and started saying stupid lines from the movie. Lisa and Renee thought this was *hi*-larious. This left me and Jimmy alone, sort of. He kicked a rock down the sidewalk, and I sat on the curb.

Lisa asked me a thousand questions after the boys left. She thought maybe Jimmy Leighton was saying lines from another movie to me. She's always hoping someone will walk out of a movie screen and talk to her like Hugh Grant talks to Julia Roberts. That would be her favorite thing in the world. But no, Jimmy Leighton didn't say a single thing to me the whole night.

We felt sorry for ourselves because it was Renee who kissed Steven Ng. We didn't actually see it happen, but she came back inside from taking another walk and looked all pink. She told us she kissed him first. After, he stood there and then skated off, saying, "Okay, see you around."

This is why Lisa decided about the French-kiss pact. She wants to look like Renee did. I tried to tell her Renee looks happy *all* the time, but no, she didn't believe me. She said a light switched on inside her eyes, a switch that comes on when you get kissed. I will have to ask Charlotte if this is so.

chapter 14

As far as I can tell, a recipe is a secret code made up of measurements. The way Charlotte is studying the King Ranch recipe, you would think she is preparing for a test. As if Casserole Man will not know she loves him if it doesn't have precisely one and a half cups of shredded cheese and a quarter teaspoon of chili powder, thank you very much. And maybe that's true. She's had her nose at the paper for some time now, so I decide to be helpful and arrange the items on the counter in alphabetical order.

Broth, cheese, chicken, rice, soup, spices, tortillas.

"Okay, we need a nine-by-thirteen casserole dish." She opens and closes cabinet doors, searching for what she needs. Her mother is away on a cruise this week, so we have the luxury of a whole house to ourselves, except for her brother. Charlotte says he won't be here much, because he's studying and has his career in pizza to worry about.

I like how her kitchen is a lot tidier than ours. The counters are pale yellow, just like the tiles on the wall behind them. The cabinets aren't solid wood but have glass in the middle so it appears you are looking into minihouses where plates live. Even though the layout of the house is similar to ours, this house feels bigger. The paneling in the living room, for example, has been painted a nice shade of sky blue.

At our house, we still have the dark brown paneling. It's like living inside a barrel. If we stay in Garland, I will try to get the courage to talk to my dad about painting the house. We could paint our paneling blue, too. Maybe keep going from the living room and down the hall and put my pink room out of its pink misery.

"First, we'll poach the chicken," Charlotte says.

"Sounds dirty."

She rolls her eyes. "What?"

"*Poach*. It sounds dirty."

"Where do you get those ideas?"

"Mostly from all the movies I'm not supposed to watch," I say. "There are a lot of bad words in good literature. I've read the books my dad assigns his students, and they have plenty of uncommon words and romance, which, if you ask me, is even stronger when it's in a book. It gets your imagi-nation all fired up."

Charlotte asks me if my dad is dating. *Dating* is a trou-ble word. He hardly ever gets past two dates.

"No one has made him a casserole yet, if that's what you mean," I tell her, wondering if there will ever be a woman bearing food for my dad, and if so, will I have to eat it? Because this King Ranch casserole doesn't look like it will be too tasty. The last woman hung around longer than any others I know about. It was a couple of months until she found out who we were. Of course, I don't know all the details, because her name is a trouble word and *"Sarah, this is none of your business."*

Well, she *was* my business when she was all happy and smiley watching movies at our house. Then she sent him an e-mail saying she'd rather not see him. I know. I read it.

Tom,
   I'm so sorry to have to write this to you on e-mail, but I can't see you again. I hope you under-stand. I've just decided I should not be dating right now.
   Deirdre

Her story might have held up if we hadn't seen her out at the movies with another man the next weekend. Of course, I wanted to walk up to her and say, *Oh, you aren't dating, huh?* That's how mad she made me. I told Dad I never liked her because her hair was some unrealistic shade of red she got out of a box and who did she think she was fooling?

I grease the baking pans while Charlotte poaches the chicken. While we wait for it to cook, I make her look up the definition of *poach* on her phone. Sure enough, the first definition has something to do with cooking, but the second one has to do with crime. You have to love a word that can do that.

poach *v.*: to cook in a hot liquid that is kept just below the boiling point; to trespass, especially on another's game preserve, in order to steal animals or to hunt

Next, she lets me shred the chicken while she checks her e-mails. Since it's a long time before she comes back into the kitchen, I decide to impress her by finishing the other steps in the recipe. I am an expert on following directions, and before you know it, I have two casseroles in the oven with time to wash the dishes.

I make my way from the kitchen to the family room to snoop around. Nothing has changed much since I was here in December. Just more pictures of Charlotte's mom on different cruises.

Like in a lot of houses in this neighborhood, there is a minibar in one corner. The back of the wall above the bar is always solid mirror with four glass shelves on top for glasses and liquor. But in Charlotte's house, the shelves are stuffed with books, which is a nice touch.

I investigate what books they have worth reading. I touch their spines as I look them over, each one holding a story inside its pages. I pull one down to read the jacket. This is something I love to do. Reading the short description inside a book, getting just enough information so you must know what happens.

Before I put the book back in its place, I catch my reflection in a small space between the books. I am an unread book, too. I am waiting to know what happens to me.

Our kitchen table rocks against the floor when you lean on it. We didn't move it here. It came with the house, which should tell you something. We have to make do with the wobbling while we eat our King Ranch casserole. Turns out, we made two casseroles so we could taste test one of them. Charlotte wants to know what a grown man thinks of the recipe, so I have to collect Dad's opinion and bring it to her tomorrow. In exchange, she is going to let me download songs for my new iPod. I still haven't told Dad about the Mr. Wistler assignment and the prize I won.

So Casserole Man has to wait another day. Until then, I am enjoying a new dinner, which is actually more tasty than I expected. My dad seems to like it, too. He keeps nodding. I hope he doesn't ask me about the Funyuns I was supposed to get and didn't and will have to make up a lie about if he does.

"So," my dad says. I can tell by the way he stretches out the "ooooo" this is his verbal entrance into a question he's wanted to ask me since dinner began. He is so obvious.

"Did you ever get a card from your mother?"

He is drinking Dr Pepper and his eyes are sad. I have to think a minute about what I can tell him, run through my mental list of trouble words. I talked to Plant, and we agreed this card was different from the others and should be thrown away. I couldn't get over the way she'd crossed out her name and written *Your Mother* as a second thought. I didn't want to take any chances he'd find it in the trash, so I threw it away in Mrs. Dupree's garbage can. But he knows. He saw the envelope on my dresser.

"It had a dog on it. A smiling dog."

He tries to investigate more. "Anything interesting

inside it? Anything about…" He does not finish his thought. I wait to see if there will be more. This might be an opportune time to slip in a question for my investigation. *Opportune* is my new favorite word, mostly for how it sounds.

opportune *adj.*: occurring or coming at an appropriate time; well-timed

"She wants to know about my new self."

"That's nice," he finally says. Then he takes a long drink and stares hard into the glass. I try to gauge if anything I said had a trouble word. He doesn't get two cards a year from her. Not since the divorce. Before, they sent e-mails once in a while, or so he said. I've never been able to find them. The last communication I saw was an official letter from the state telling us they'd moved her to a hospital in Wichita Falls.

"Want to play Scrabble?" I offer, trying to lighten the mood.

"Maybe one game. I've got all those papers to grade." His look is still far away, his mind traveling to another place.

"Why don't I make you coffee and you can start grading now? I'd rather go sit outside and look at the trees anyway."

"Yeah? I think you are trying to spy on the neighborhood."

"Well, sometimes that just happens when you are looking at trees." How does he know I am a spy? I will have to work on being more stealth, which is also my new favorite word.

stealth *adj.*: surreptitious; secret; not openly acknowledged

He touches my cheek in that tender way and smiles. It's good I have the soft kind of dad today. It makes up for a lot of things.

"Tell Charlotte this was exceptional," he says.

I clear the table, wash dishes, and think about how it might be if I ever have someone to cook a casserole for one day. Why go to all the fuss when you could order a pizza and wouldn't have to clean the kitchen? But if I do ever have someone special to cook for, I will get a nicer set of plates. Ours all have chipped edges.

I go and get Plant, and we sit on the front-porch step and look at the night. Sunset isn't until eight thirty, so the sky looks dirty blue. I pick at the weeds coming up in the cracks of the walk and wish it was completely dark.

I want to walk around the neighborhood and look in

other people's windows and see what they ⟨ ⟩ course, Charlotte is likely saying lovey-d⟨ ⟩ Casserole Man. And the Duprees, well, ⟨ ⟩ go for a walk when it gets darker and cooler, so I mig⟨ ⟩ them in person. A few times, I've spotted Mrs. Dupree standing at her kitchen window and wondered what they had for dinner. When I threw my birthday card in her trash, I noticed an empty can of tomato sauce, so maybe they are enjoying spaghetti tonight.

There it is, the sting of being alone. Why do I do this, sitting here imagining other people's lives?

I tell myself to shut up, be happy, you are getting the summer you wanted. You would be more alone in Houston with your grandparents. Putting up with Casserole Man isn't so bad. Well. The whole situation feels somehow out of whack. Like the bed still unmade at two o'clock in the afternoon and so the whole day feels messy. When I get to feeling like this, I wish I had someone to talk to. Like a mom.

Dear Atticus,
I would like to begin this letter with an apology. You always say that it is more polite to get a person talking about what they are interested in rather than what you are interested in. Here I am, writing all this stuff, asking your opinions, and I have not

talked to you about your interests. Here's what I know you like:

- You read the newspapers every day.
- You are a lawyer.
- You were called One-Shot Finch because of your shooting skills.
- You read every night.
- You do not drink.
- You prefer to walk to your job.

I admire all of these things about you, Atticus. If you could somehow come into my world today, I would lay out the newspapers for you, but I'd have to tell you that there is so much news you can find on the Internet, which is a window to the world on a computer screen. There, you could find out about the news all over the planet. I imagine you would still prefer to read the actual newspaper in your hands. I am the same way. My best friend, Lisa, just got a new e-reader, which is a thin, electronic, dessert-plate-sized substitute for a book. You wouldn't like it.

Also, I'd love to walk with you. I would show you our town, though there is not much to it. The houses in our neighborhood don't have porches.

Or really, not the kind of porches you have in May-comb, where you can be a back-porch listener, like your sister. (I think I would be a back-porch listener if I could.) Here, the porches are tiny square concrete things that are only good for the UPS guy to leave a package on or for a guy to give you a quick kiss good night. They are not built for having a long conversation on or for putting a cot out on to sleep, though I think I might try this one night just to see. You'd probably like the downtown part of town the best, which has a square, little shops, a fountain, and lots of benches that no one actually sits on. I am not sure what else is interesting about Garland that I could show you. I will have to find out. There must be something. My own dad works at a community college too far to walk to. That is too bad. He'd talk to me more if we walked some-place together, don't you think? He does read a lot, too, but then he drinks until he's drunk, so that sort of cancels out that good thing.

Sincerely,
Sarah Nelson

chapter 15

Here I am on Charlotte's front porch, waiting for her to answer the doorbell. We are going to have a girls' day today with nail polish, movies, and popcorn. Then I am giving her twenty dollars of my birthday money and she will help me add songs to my new iPod. I love this day. I will pretend we are sisters. I'd like to think no one knows you better than a sister. And there are only some people you want to paint your toes in front of anyway.

The screen door squeaks open, and there is a guy in flannel pants and a green T-shirt.

"Um, is Charlotte here?" I ask.

"Come on in." He smiles and runs a hand through his light brown hair. "She'll be out in a sec."

I'm pretty sure this is the pizza-delivery brother, who

I barely recognize because last summer he always had on a red ball cap with a giant pepperoni on the front.

He is younger than Charlotte by about a year, so that would make him nineteen now. I have to turn my head away quick when I realize I'm studying him. Is everyone in this family perfect-looking? Some people have the kind of eyes you never forget. His eyes are like that. If perfect is a color, it is this shade of blue.

"I'm Finn, remember?" he says, putting his hand out for me to shake. "Sarah, right?"

Charlotte appears then, still in her purple bathrobe.

"Is it time for you already?" she asks.

"Geez, Charlotte, nice," Finn says.

"Shut up, Finn."

"I can wait outside," I say.

"No," she says. "I was working late, late, late."

Inside the house, I try to glance in the mirror without it being obvious I'm checking out my blotchy neck. I've set a record for blushing, staring at Finn so long, but when someone is nice to look at it's hard to turn away.

I follow Charlotte into the kitchen. The wonderful smell of coffee fills the air. It smells better here for some reason. She stretches and yawns, and then a new kind of smile fans out on her face.

"Well, I wasn't working the entire night," she says as if

99

to answer the question mark on my face. "I was up late on the phone with Christopher."

"Who?"

"The guy," she says. "The one I told you about."

Casserole Man is named Christopher.

"Oh. How long did you talk to him?"

"Forever," Finn says. She cuffs his head as he pours himself a cup of coffee.

"Don't you have to go to work?" she says.

"I'm here for your entertainment," he replies.

"Watch this, Sarah," she says. "Finn is a human dictionary. I told him about your word obsession. You won't need me to look anything up for you. Give him a word."

"A word?" I am wondering how it is that I have a word obsession and if this is a good sign.

"Anything."

I should come up with something clever and strange, but then he'd be expecting that. A common word will stump him, I just know it. So I choose.

"How about *forever*, then?"

And Finn says, "Everlasting. Eternal. Evermore. As in Charlotte was on the phone *forever*."

"At least I have a life and I'm not a dork," she replies.

"Umm-hmm," Finn says. "Great comeback. Don't worry. I'll be out of your hair products in an hour."

I am half wondering what two people can talk about

for hours, but then I have talked to Lisa for hours at the mall about how some clothes should come in only certain sizes and should not have words on them if their butt is too wide. I wonder if these are the topics Charlotte and Casserole Man talked about. Probably not.

"Are we going to paint our nails first?" she asks.

"Remember last year when we painted each nail a different color?"

"Yeah, I don't like that anymore," she says.

I feel my face go hot.

"Yeah, me neither," I lie. I still want each toe a different color. Now I'll do this only in the wintertime, when my toes are safe from ridicule.

I sit on the floor of her room and line up all the bottles of nail polish, starting with the lightest color, Ballet Pink, and ending with the richest shade, Frankly, Scarlett. After we finish painting our toes, we'll put on our flip-flops and let the polish dry while we pick out my songs. Then we'll make peanut butter and jelly with the crusts off, or maybe there is free pizza. Charlotte will go and work on her thesis paper while I watch a movie and make us snacks and think more about the Mr. Wistler assignment. Sure, I know I don't have to keep writing to win the iPod, but I feel like I need to, so I brought my composition book with me. Maybe this is part of my word obsession.

Charlotte changed from her bathrobe into a floaty

white shirt and skirt. Her hair is pulled back with a navy-blue headband. She looks like a face-soap model. I make a mental note to peek in her bathroom later when she's working and write down her brand of soap.

We set up our polish stations on two different stools and get to work. She is so nice and lets me paint her toes first. Then she just casually says, "Tell me something about you I don't know."

I think about just blurting out the first thing on my brain.

I got a card from my mother.

I picture the words hanging in the air, swinging a little.

Charlotte thinks my mother is dead. She doesn't know I'm a twin, or supposed to be. We could leave this lie alone, though I would like to tell her, to confess, to have a confidante who might pinch me when I show signs of crazy. Tell me to concentrate on normal thoughts like accessories and casseroles.

As I dip the brush into the nail polish, I decide to let my mother remain dead. I know Charlotte would be a good friend about the whole subject, but I can't risk that she would look at me the sad way people do before they say good-bye.

"I smoked a bunch of cigarettes this year," I lie. "And I am close to having my first French kiss." I don't tell her about the bet with Lisa yet. She should be impressed I came up with this on my own.

"And being kissed back, I suppose," Charlotte says, completing my imaginary sentence. For the moment, I just shrug my shoulders. The image of someone's lips on mine flashes before me, though I can't see the face to go with the other set of lips.

"What else don't I know about you?" she asks.

"Nothing."

My brother's name is Simon. I'm the one who is here, alive to even tell lies. My mother is not dead, just unreachable. My father drinks. I have two diaries. I talk to a plant. I'm afraid of doing a Family Tree Project and am trying to figure out how I can skip seventh grade.

"I'm so glad it's summer," Charlotte says. "It's nice to come home to your same, comfy bed. The one I have at school is gross."

"I guess so."

"I can never get my laundry to smell the same as when my mother does it."

I don't have any memory of my mother washing my clothes, but my dad does a decent job. I have always washed the light-colored clothes while dad washes the dark. It isn't much fun unless Dad decides it is a good day to have a sock fight. A sock fight is when you ball up two socks together and throw them at your opponent.

I've given each of Charlotte's toes a glossy coat of Frankly, Scarlett. It's not the best job I've ever done. My hand was a bit shaky, feeling Charlotte's puzzled face all over me.

"Please don't tell my father about the smoking. He will have a cow." This wasn't a lie. It was the truth. Dad likes to imagine me safe and under glass, away from smoke and boys. If he knew what kids talked about on the bus, I would have my own private chauffeur to school, that is certain.

"I won't tell a soul," she says, placing a finger on the bottle of Ballet Pink polish. "What we say is in the vault of secrets."

As often happens with my brain, I picture an actual vault of secrets. It is wide and gray, and there is a cute security guard next to it who happens to look exactly like Jimmy Leighton. He spins the giant golden lock on the door. The guard tosses an envelope carrying a secret inside the vault. He closes the door quickly before any secrets can escape. As he puts his back to the door, you can hear the sound of hands knocking on the other side, the secrets begging to come out.

This is what I am. A vault of secrets. They flutter inside my chest like caged birds, wanting to take flight but afraid to fly.

chapter 16

The whole day that I had planned put on wings and flew out the window as soon as Charlotte said Casserole Man was coming over. I think I read in a magazine that women will "throw over" their friends if there is a man in their life. Now I know it is true. I feel thrown.

I peek out Charlotte's bedroom window and see her embrace him on the front walk. He is so tall I bet he will fill a doorway. He has sandy hair and a bushy mustache to match. And he is wearing cowboy boots with an intricate embroidered design. Who does he think he is, wearing boots in the summertime?

They hug and kiss. It's hard to tell if she is getting kissed back at this angle. I wait in the bedroom until I hear the squeak of the screen door. I count to ten before entering the living room in case there is more kissing to be done. But no, that is not happening, because Finn is sitting on the couch and I'm sure it would be awkward to make out in front of your own brother.

"That's my younger brother, Finn," Charlotte says.

"I didn't even know you had a brother," Casserole Man says.

"Well, he's only around because my mother isn't here," Charlotte says. Finn gives her a look.

"This is Sarah, the friend I told you about." Now I know something is different about her. She is being so formal.

Christopher extends his hand, too, so I take it. He shakes it firm and sure.

"She wants to have her first kiss this summer," Charlotte adds. My face grows hot and prickly, my mouth dry. Where is the vault security guard now? On a coffee break? She is telling her brother and her boyfriend things about me as if I'm not here.

I don't mean to look at Finn, but I do. He winks at me, which makes my face go redder. It probably matches Frankly, Scarlett.

"So, what are we going to do today?" Casserole Man asks.

Charlotte asks if we wouldn't all like to take a walk around the block first. Well, this is going to do nothing for my freshly painted toes, which I had to do by myself, thank you very little! I'm feeling less girlie already, and I guess it shows in my shoulders because Christopher shakes one of them and says, "Hey, why do you stand on the stump in your yard?"

All three of them look at me like I'm a museum exhibit and there is a card at my feet reading: *Girl Who Stands on Stump*.

If a tornado struck Garland right now, I wouldn't mind. It could pick me up and set me down in a new place where I don't know anyone. I could start fresh, just be known as Tornado Girl.

I don't like the fact that Casserole Man knows something about me. And then Charlotte and Christopher are holding hands, and it's clear to me I will be trailing behind them. I wish we didn't make King Ranch casserole so good. He does not deserve it.

"Do you know Charlotte is planning to get a PhD?" I ask, trying to change the subject.

And he responds, "Yes, I do know that."

"So she's smart. Smarter than most. What are you studying?" I put the emphasis on *you* with double italics.

"Business."

"And that's how you got the big job at Wilson's Western Wear?"

Finn laughs.

"Shut up, Finn, and go read your girlfriend, the

107

dictionary!" Charlotte shouts, but he keeps right on laughing. I hope he doesn't stop, it sounds that nice.

Then she informs me they'll be right back after their walk. Alone. Fine by me. Go walk with a fake, casserole-eating cowboy, for all I care. They are outside before you can say "boo."

"Why'd she call the dictionary your girlfriend?" I ask Finn.

"Because I love words," he says. "I'm sure she means it that way, anyway."

"Oh, cool." I don't want him to think I think this is a bad thing.

"A lot of people don't think so, but, hey, I got a scholarship to college because of it, and she is jealous."

"Really?" I didn't know reading a book could lead to a college education.

"Nerd alert!" he says. "You're looking at a bona fide spelling bee champion. I have the flash cards to prove it."

Well, that is something. All I can say to this is one lousy "Wow."

"Yep. Now I'm in my junior year at college as a linguistics and etymology major. Do you know what that is?"

"My father is a professor, so it's a safe bet I know a lot of things," I tell him, which is true. I am familiar with all the -ologys a person can learn about.

He looks at me, cocking his head to the side, then says,

"Good to know. Good to know. Well, that's why she makes fun of my degree sometimes. You know how sisters can be."

"No, not really."

"Then you're lucky," Finn says.

"I've never met anyone else who liked to read the dictionary," I tell him.

"Oh, so you are one of us, eh? There aren't many of us, I can tell you," he says. "Turn back now before it's too late."

"What?"

"Never mind."

"Do you still deliver pizza?"

"Yes."

"Good."

And this is the end of our conversation because here come the lovebirds again. As he goes by, Christopher rubs my head. Does he think I'm a pet? He tells me that Charlotte forgot her purse. What a person needs a purse for on a walk, I have no idea. My dislike for him is growing, but I will try to make my face look pleasant anyway and make small talk.

"So what's the story about you and casseroles anyway? That's funeral food," I say.

Christopher's expression is one I imagine he has when he can't solve a math problem. He doesn't look like a brainiac to me.

"Yes, Sarah helped me with some recipes yesterday. In

fact," she says, tugging me toward the kitchen, "I need to talk to her about something recipe-related."

She drags me to the dining room.

"The fact that I made him a casserole was a secret," she says, taking a brush from her purse, running it through the snarls in my hair. I hate to brush it myself. "I should have told you before. I'm trying to impress him."

"Telling people I stand on a tree stump and wanted a first kiss was *also* a secret," I say, which makes her laugh.

I tell her, "Well, you definitely picked the right nail color. He should be impressed with that. But I think he doesn't realize you are so smart."

"How can you tell?" she asks.

It's obvious to me, but I tell her what she should look for and ask, "How many questions has he asked *you* today?"

She considers my question. "That doesn't mean anything."

If she only had the benefit of my father's wisdom. He always said one well-put question shows more intelligence and interest than two paragraphs of talk.

"We're going out again. I need ink for my printer. Finn will watch you."

"I don't need to be watched."

She whispers in my ear, "Be good and I'll tell you everything when I get back."

I suppose this is the best I can hope for today. I need to collect real-life information and compare it with what I've read in *The Valiant Rake*. Right now I'm rereading a chapter where Rebecca tells the rake that she hates him and that loving him is the worst thing she could ever do. Then she kisses him, which is not exactly smart on her part.

By the time they've reached the sidewalk, they are holding hands, their shoulders brushing together as they go. They look straight at each other as they walk, and if they aren't careful, they will run into a tree or trip over the curb. Lisa is wrong about kissing and love. It might make you pretty at first, but it makes you look stupid, too.

I sit on a white plastic chair on Charlotte's porch, or what passes for a porch. It is already warmed by the sun. While my toes dry properly, I take a good look at the neighborhood. I never saw the Duprees go for a walk last night, and Mr. Dupree's long green car is still parked in front of his house. It makes me consider the possible options: sick, overslept, dead. There are other, less likely possibilities, too: alien abduction, vacation, movie marathon. In crime shows, an investigator will sometimes put chalk lines on car tires to monitor movement.

I'll go home early today, find some chalk, then take care of myself, thank you very much. Our fridge is stocked with actual food right now. There is something on every shelf. Grandma always leaves it that way, and not just with carrots.

Her upper lip is red when she gets back. I know it's from kissing bushy mustache hair. If you want to know, I suspect Charlotte is dating a real-life rake.

The lovebirds pretend not to notice me as they go inside, still hand in hand. What I'm thinking is *Whatever*. I look at a magazine and pick out the girls I want to look like. This is something Lisa and I used to do, even though we knew it was no use — we'd never look that good in a million years. There is one girl I particularly admire because her hair is short and blunt-cut like mine. She wears a thick, dark choker necklace and long, teardrop-shaped earrings. These would look good on me for certain. There's an article on the opposite page.

Five Ways to Appear More Confident
Swing your shoulders way back.
Count to three before responding to someone's question.
Cross your legs at the ankle when seated.
Ask the person opposite you what they've been reading.
Make direct eye contact.

Finn lets the screen door slam shut and sits down on the other plastic chair. He puts his bare feet up on the railing and laces his hands behind his head. I notice that the hems of his jeans are worn out from being dragged around. This is a sign he's been to a lot of places.

I fan myself with the magazine the way I've seen the women in movies do.

"I thought you liked to read," Finn says, not even looking at me, so I can't make direct eye contact. It's a struggle, but I manage to count to three before responding.

I say, "This *is* reading," waving the magazine in case he has poor eyesight and can't see how obviously wrong he is.

"I meant a book."

I know where he's trying to steer this talk about books over magazines, but if he only knew me, he would know I've outread most kids my age. Especially if you count the book summaries in my dad's college-essay assignments. And, yes, there are loads of books I haven't read, but I can wait. Books don't go bad. They don't spoil on you like milk you have to drink before the expiration date.

"So, what have *you* been reading, then?" I ask.

He takes his legs down, sits up at attention.

"*Ulysses* by James Joyce," he says. "Ever heard of it?"

"My father has a copy, though I've never read it myself. He says it will be more enjoyable after I've read Homer."

"Okaaay," he says, in a way I can tell means he's impressed. There. I have it. The magazine was right. My father always gives me a hard time about magazines, but now I have evidence of their effectiveness.

"Don't you have something to study? Or are you a slacker?"

I hope this makes him go inside and leave me to my thoughts about Mr. Dupree's car and where is the best place to make the chalk marks, front or back?

He laughs. "Well, I do have my whole pizza career, as you know. And I've written a huge paper, and it's being edited now. While my mom's gone, I'm trying to chill out for a while. Hence, evidence of being a slacker. But right now I'm just waiting for a FedEx."

He says this so plainly and sweetly I am all of a sudden embarrassed at my questions. Plus, I don't think I've met another person in real life, besides my dad, who uses the word *hence*.

"So, why do you stand on the tree stump?"

"You've seen me?" I ask. This is so embarrassing.

He thinks on this a minute and then says, "Don't you look at something you've never seen before?" I guess I do. All this time I've watched everyone else in our neighborhood and I had no clue someone might be watching me.

He gets a far-off look in his eyes, smiles right into the sun. His brain is traveling someplace nice, I just know it. I get a nice view of him in profile. He could be in a magazine, easy. Maybe an ad for cologne or something. Wouldn't I love to have a camera right now? Yes, I would.

Dear Atticus,

Today I am feeling strange and don't really know what to say. I've tried to think how to seek your advice about my own mother. To do that, I realize that I must tell you all about her. This will be the TMI (too much information) letter. I almost don't want to write it in case someone discovers these letters. If they do, I am in deep trouble. I've already gotten called names because of my situation. And we've moved around a lot because of it. But I remembered what you said to Jem about people who called *you* bad names, names I cannot even repeat here. Remember that time? You told Jem that it's not an insult for someone to call you what *they* think is a bad name. Atticus, I don't want to hurt your feelings, but I'm not sure if I believe that. Anyway, I will tell you about my mother and get it out of the way.

Here goes. The situation with my mother is this: She went crazy ten years ago. Now, before you tell me I'm using my imagination and that she is just like Arthur Radley next door, no, she is not. She is a real-life crazy person who lives in a mental institution because she killed my brother and tried to kill me. There was a big trial about it, too. Two trials, actually: one for her and one for my father, who was charged with something I don't completely understand.

So you see, I don't have a relationship with my mother. I am not quite as lucky as Scout in this area. Scout's mother, your wife, died when Scout was two, and so she doesn't remember her. And because you are such a good father, your kids don't miss her. (Plus, they have Calpurnia making them mind and cooking meals, which must be nice.) For me, I have none of these things. No mother. No brother. No Calpurnia. And a dad who is there, but not there.

And I just realized this, but I know my mother more as Jane Nelson, a sort of famous person who embarrasses me. Anytime I hear the name *Jane*, my head snaps around and I start to turn red. You shouldn't be ashamed of your own mother's name, should you? You would probably tell me I am a low person for thinking that. I will try to improve.

Sincerely,
Sarah Nelson

chapter 17

Dad is grading papers in the living room tonight, singing some Beatles song. He gets stuck on one old singing group at a time, and that's all you will hear, twenty-four seven. It was Bob Seger for a while, and now here we are with John, Paul, George, and Ringo.

I go into my room and wonder how a brain remembers lyrics without writing everything down. How it decides which things to keep, which to forget. There must be little memories stuck inside a mind like gum under a table. It takes some elbow grease to get them off, so you have to want them gone or they'll be there forever, dried up and hard. Sometimes memories pop up out of nowhere, and you have to trace your steps, figure out how your mind got thinking about a certain thing. Dr. Madrigal said this is sometimes called a trigger.

For example, right now I look at the bumpy ceiling in my room and all I can think about are white summer sandals. Why? Because earlier today, I saw a little girl in white sandals running down the sidewalk, chasing after the ice-cream truck. She looked back and shouted to her dad, "Hurry up! Hurry up! We're going to miss it!" It was so funny because the ice-cream truck drives slower than a person riding a bike. Still, she was getting all worked up, thinking she was going to miss getting an orange Dreamsicle or something.

Well, just seeing that little girl was a trigger to a memory of my mother. Snap your fingers. It was just like that. Here's what my brain pulled out of a file:

1.   I had those same white summer sandals, which buckled at my ankle.
2.   I wore them to the hospital to see my mother.
3.   Dad hid me under his coat as we walked from the hospital to the car. He said, "I've got you. Just watch your feet."
4.   I watched white-sandaled feet move across the hot black asphalt parking lot.

Why didn't I have enough sense to keep a diary back then? I would be able to remember more, like was I six or seven when that happened? Had I visited her before that day? How many times have I seen her in real life since then? Two? Three? And was this the time I'd announced to my class friends, "Hey, my mom lives in a hospital and can't live with me"? Maybe I was six. When you are six, you tell everything. I know I told a girl I was leaving school early to go see my mom at the hospital, and she told me she watched her mom pee in a cup at the doctor's office.

Later, when you are seven, you realize this information will come back to you in a mean way. Then you learn how much to tell, when to lie, when not to say anything. By the time you are eight, your secrets are locked in your diary.

Now, I think about that day in private. The details ache to get out. This is one reason I love Plant. She is a good listener, patient and kind. Right now, I tell her my mind won't let me loose until I think up some new fact, some new scene. It's as if my brain computer is putting together a puzzle, but some pieces are lost. Plant wonders if this is because of all the questions counselors asked me. Maybe they put in pieces that weren't there in the first place. Maybe they invent triggers. I don't know.

I tell Plant that the time I had on white sandals was right after Dad's trial. We had our eye on moving away because everyone knew us from the newspapers. Sometimes they did the undercover technique, which is where they pretend to be a friendly neighbor and then start being nosy.

Because of the undercover people, Dad kep

e whenever we walked to our car in our neighbor-
in a parking lot. Yes, that is when I stared at my
feet in sandals, walking fast. Anytime I smell his deodor-
ant, I think of being chased by reporters. So when he asked
me over pancakes and bacon if I wanted to move someplace where it would just be the two of us, I said, "Heck,
yes." Well, I didn't actually say *heck*. I said the other word.
He frowned and said it was clear I'd been spending too
much time around Gramps and would I please not use that
word? It was one of the first trouble words.

And now, I remember more. I tell Plant this was the time
Dad said, "Hey, we're going to the hospital to see your
mother. She may or may not talk to you today, but you
remember she still loves you, even if she doesn't look at
you, okay?"

So we went.

At the hospital, the doctor said, "Hey, there she is with the
light brown hair and blue eyes. She is your mother." I
remember not wanting to go up to her because I was
afraid.

I remember the doctor led me and Dad to a small
room with a table and several chairs. There was a giant rug
made up of multicolored blocks on the floor.

I remember she rubbed her palms on her plain blue

pants and kept smoothing them even though there were no wrinkles.

I remember handing her a card I'd made her. Actually, it was a card Dad told me I should make for her. It wasn't my idea. When she didn't reach for it, I placed it on the table and backed away.

I remember Dad telling me to go play outside the room, the only problem being there is no place to go play at a mental hospital. I stepped outside the door and sat alone in the hallway, picking at the carpet.

Plant is still listening, so I keep talking.

What else do I remember? I don't know.

I wonder if I'm adding those details in the way a little kid colors a page, scribbling all outside the lines. It becomes the picture you make it. And no one can tell you if it's right or wrong. I wish I had a photograph of that day. It would show hard evidence that this visit actually took place the way I think it did. Hard evidence is when you have something that is so true you can't argue with it.

The only hard evidence I have is this: I remember I wore white summer sandals when I saw her. That is all I know for sure.

chapter 18

Plant thinks I am wrong, but I'm ignoring her. I told her I'd been worried that I might also turn out like my father and become an alcoholic. I got my dictionary out and read aloud:

alcoholic *n*.: a person who drinks alcoholic substances habitually and to excess

I am not an alcoholic, I tell her, because I do not drink. That is a relief. I might turn out crazy like my mom and not be able to help it. But a person can help it if they pour themselves a drink. As long as I do not do that, I can mark *alcoholic* off my list of things that will happen to me. But then my brain gives me a good argument. If my mother is crazy and my dad is, by definition, an alcoholic, then I

would rather become more like him. Any fool wour̩
choose Jim Beam over crazy. And Plant said I was crazy
because I was talking to her.

She has a point.

I write these thoughts in my real diary so I can work
that out later. Superquick, I grab my fake diary and write
a few lines about wanting to enter a spelling bee. Then I
stare up at the ceiling fan and pound out its wobbly
rhythm on my mattress. I'm in bed thinking about the day
and trying to think up a good lie to tell Lisa in case I can't
find someone to kiss. She doesn't know what a good liar I
am. I could say he had a mustache and tell her my lip got
all red. I shut this idea out because it makes my brain feel
as if it's trying to solve a mathematical word problem and
can't find the answer. And now I'm fully awake.

Dad is still up late, too, watching a Western on TV.
Sounds of shoot-outs travel down the hall and into my
room. I have to wonder what kind of pioneer or cowboy
came to Garland and thought, *Hey, this flat land looks
great. Let's make our camp here and get to work.* His wife, a
woman in a shawl with a small child in her arms, would
ask, *Is it safe to stay here?* And he'd respond, *Sure, who else
is going to fight us for this, anyway? I don't see anyone around
for miles.* And so began a long history of people who
don't care where they put down roots. I can't think of any
other reason Garland exists. This town is like a gray

does its job all right, but it's no fashion

eel a warmth crawl up my neck at the thought of how silly I acted in front of Finn. I wonder if he can tell me more about what boys do. Help fill in some gaps of knowledge. Maybe I'll find there are things to admire about them, though I am doubtful. They are usually smelly and rude and just won't open car doors for you, which is a trait Gramps says I should be on the lookout for.

Be on the lookout for boys who don't open car doors.

Be on the lookout for boys who wear their hair too long. What the heck are they hiding? (I don't have to tell you that he didn't say *heck*.)

Be on the lookout for nice-quality sweaters that can last more than one season.

Be on the lookout for free dinners.

Being on the lookout is big for Gramps.

I sit up in bed and try to figure out if there's something I forgot to do. Did I forget to water Plant? Or leave my clothes in the dryer? Then I realize I forgot to put the chalk marks on Mr. Dupree's tires. Maybe this is it.

My thoughts are interrupted by the sound of a horse. And since I know there is not one in our kitchen, I let my feet hit the floor and go to investigate. It is only my dad, now heavily asleep on the sofa with a college paper on his chest, the Western blaring from the TV.

I take the paper from my dad's hand and then cover him with a blanket. I'll let him sleep soundly here, where he ends up many nights anyway. His eyes twitch beneath his lids, so I know he's in a powerful dream. Maybe he's riding a wild horse, trying to keep up with a cowboy. Well, let him dream.

I find the rest of the students' papers and stack them neatly on the coffee table, the most recently read one on top, turned askew. Something in the first paragraph leaps off the page:

If she had wanted to, she would have. She would have continued to pursue the work before her, earnestly and intently. Instead, she left it behind and never once looked back again. Her talents heretofore unused dried up like a crisp fall leaf.

F.

I would give this a big fat F. The reader has no idea what work or talents *she* has or had or left behind. My father always says a good piece should be understood by a twelve-year-old. Now I see what he means. I cannot make sense of this at all, and I'm already too bored to keep reading. This must be what put my father to sleep. He says most of his students write as if they just discovered Shakespeare and the dictionary on the same day.

A sound of two glasses clinking together comes from my father's computer down the hall. I go into his office and spy a small yellow box at the bottom of the screen with a question mark blinking. I sit in his office chair and have a look. It's a message from PBroom —*Are you still online?*

Who is PBroom and how does my father know how to do these things? Like Mr. Wistler, Dad is an antitexter. I see the cursor blinking and cannot resist. It's as if it's saying *Answer Now Answer Now.* I type *Yes* and hit enter. The computer makes the glass-clinking sound again. Up pops another message from PBroom, and I can't help but answer.

I can't sleep either. What are you doing?
Grading papers.
Ugh. Sounds fun.
Yeah. There's a stupefyingly bad one. I want to give it an F.
Ouch! That's harsh.
Well.
Coffee was fun the other day. As always.
Yes.
I think you're spoiling me.
LOL. I've got to go.
Good night.

And PBroom is gone. I scan the instant chat again. There are so many questions. He's had coffee with PBroom. He or *she* knows how to reach him through instant message. He/she is thinking of him at this time of night. Worse, he would *never* use "LOL" in a message. I am totally busted.

I hear two cowboys having a confrontation in the living room. This is my father's favorite part, so I leave it on, let it sink good and well into his dreamtime. Maybe he'll wake up tomorrow and feel heroic. He'll picture himself as one of the old-fashioned good guys. And then I'll make him superstrong, black cowboy coffee and buttered toast and send him back out into the world to fight another day. Ha-ha! And I can find a way to ask him about PBroom without sounding like I know anything. Without sounding like I pretended to be him for sixty seconds.

On the way back to my room, I take a detour and — voilà — I am in the garage. It's as if my feet took me here and didn't tell my brain. The bottles are behind the paint cans. I don't know why he hides them there. It's not as if both of us don't know he drinks. I pull out a half-full bottle. I unscrew the cap and think about taking a sip. I just sniff it, though, and it's awful. The smell of it almost burns my nose. I still don't see why he drinks this.

By the time I get to my room, a shameful feeling rises up. I almost took a drink! And I pretended to be my dad on the computer. I have to wonder if this is a part of the new me. A criminal.

There on my pillow is my green composition book, and I know Atticus would look at me over the top of his glasses and I would feel his precise disappointment, all in one look. Atticus would make a great cowboy. I picture him wearing a wide-brimmed hat and one of those long coats, maybe a shiny sheriff's badge. *You know right from wrong,* he would say. And that would be enough to make you bite your lip to keep from crying.

chapter 19

I hate our house, and I think it hates me.

On mornings when I want to sleep late, the pipes in my dad's shower whistle at a high pitch until the water is warm. I sit up in bed and then remember it's summertime and I don't have to hurry. At least I have the luxury of keeping my pajamas on for a while. Still, I want to be the first one in the kitchen in the mornings. It's a tiny thrill to arrive somewhere before anyone else, like you might be the first to make a discovery and everyone will cheer you. *Hey, you were the first here. That's amazing!* This is my house, and I claim it when I can.

I toast a frozen waffle. My father and I like peanut butter and syrup on our waffles, so I decide this is what I will make today. Get his day off to a good start before I ask any questions. Plus, I have a big day ahead as I investigate what is happening with the Duprees. The morning already has palpable electricity in it. *Palpable* is my current favorite word.

palpable *adj.*: capable of being touched or felt; tangible

Anything could happen. It's not even seven o'clock yet. The day still has to make an appearance. But there is one thing I do know about it: Today is the first day I will have a cup of coffee. I worked out that coffee is the opposite of alcohol, so I am going to go that direction.

He comes into the kitchen, and I put out his favorite mug, a small blue one with a flying dog. I'm good at making coffee now. I pour him a full cup. Then a full cup for me. He just looks at me and nods like he knows it's a good decision.

"Thanks, sweetheart," he says. "Coffee is just what I need."

Yes, it sure is, I think.

"You fell asleep watching TV."

"Thanks for the blanket."

"You're welcome," I say. "I was thinking of pork chops tonight. With stuffing on the side."

"Sounds good, kiddo," he says, drinking his coffee. It makes him look peaceful the way he half closes his eyes when the mug reaches his face. "What are you doing today?"

"I don't know," I say. "Just hanging out, I guess." I take a big sip of coffee. I try to look peaceful like him, but it is so bitter and hot. I choke it down anyway. This is just what I must do.

He says, "You'll remember to tell Charlotte I'll need to talk with her brother this week."

"He's no big deal. He's studying words at college or something. Plus, he stays in his room because Charlotte is crazy in love with her boyfriend and it annoys him."

He tosses me his skeptical look, the one that brings his eyebrows low to his eyes.

"Crazy in love, huh," he says.

Now I try to correct what I've said. "Well, not *crazy* in love. He respects how hard she's working on her thesis and all." There. That should do it. Except I did use the word *crazy* again. I pour a nice dose of syrup over his waffles, hoping this will help change the subject.

"Mmm-hmmm" is all he says. This means I will have to allow him to meet Christopher, too.

"I don't think Charlotte's brother will be around much," I say. "He delivers pizza, too."

"Where does he go to school?"

"I don't know," I say. "Why do you have so many questions?"

131

"I just want to know who you're hanging out with, Sarah," he says. "Tell Charlotte I'll be calling her today."

"Dad!" If I protest, it will make it worse. I already know their conversation will be a game show of a thousand questions Finn will never answer correctly. My dad is getting in his Secret Service mode again.

"And I'll have some questions for the boyfriend, too."

"Seriously, you don't need to do that."

"Well, you wouldn't want to have to go to your grandparents'."

It's sharp the way he says this, and it just gets to me between my ribs. Words fall out of me before I get the chance to imagine myself saying them. "Who is PBroom?"

The air holds still between us. An invisible rope hangs there, and each of us waits for the other to tug it a little. I must look as surprised as he does at this moment. I take another long drink of coffee. Show him I am older.

"I guess I shouldn't be surprised that you find out these things, Sarah," he says. "Ms. Broom is a colleague of mine. She teaches American History."

"She sent you an instant message on the computer last night," I say, then quickly throw in, "when I was cleaning up the house and stuff."

They've had lunch and coffee several times. He would call them "good friends." He wants to know if any of this bothers me. Of course, he's dated women before and it didn't work out well. So it makes me wonder why he even wants to try at all. So many of the women he's taken for coffee or tea or even a taco at Taco Bell have been nice at first. Then he tells them about me, and things seem to go cloudy. I am doubtful PBroom is any different.

"Is it serious?" I ask finally.

"No," he says, and I note a small turned-up expression around his eyes. He likes her, that's for sure. She must be pretty.

"Well, I think I'd need to meet this young lady if you're going to spend so much time with her," I say.

He puts his dish in the sink and washes his hands. "I'll get the pork chops on my way home."

When I tell Plant about this later, we both agree *PBroom* might be a trouble word. I write it down in my diary, adding it to the list. There are twenty-three trouble words so far.

chapter 20

Today would be an ordinary day if not for two things: I got my period, and my dad interviewed Finn.

But I didn't know this when I walked to Charlotte's house. I'd decided today was the day to solve the mystery of the Duprees' car. Right away, I see the Duprees' car still hasn't moved.

Next time I go to Walgreens, I am going to get a little notebook, the size of a shirt pocket. Also, a disposable camera. I need to track these details in case something is wrong. My gut instinct, which is what cops have about certain situations, tells me something is wrong.

The thing I already know about the Duprees is that they used to own a green-apple orchard in California, which is interesting because apple green is the color of Mr. Dupree's car and Mrs. Dupree's kitchen countertops.

I've only ever been inside their house once, when they invited me and my father to choose a box of apples.

They never actually lived near the orchard, but they had apples sent to them all the time in big wooden crates, each one individually wrapped in paper the color of brown sugar. Mrs. Dupree said they sold the business to their son after they retired. She said Mr. Dupree still worked in produce, but at the local farmers' market. They are always giving everyone colorful fruit and vegetables they can't sell the next day, mostly because of how it looks. But Mrs. Dupree tells me it's still good, just to peel off the outside layers and find the good stuff underneath. It also worked when she met Mr. Dupree. She said he was good underneath and solid as a ripe melon.

When Mr. Dupree leaves each morning, his exit is the same as all the others as they leave the cul-de-sac in a parade of cars. And also, they always pick up their newspapers. Not that I am spying on them or anything. Today, walking across the street to Charlotte's, I spot two papers on the lawn. There is a long blue flyer hanging from the front door as well. And the apple-green car is still there, parked at the same angle as yesterday. There is much to do today: find out about the Duprees, download music to my iPod, ask Charlotte to look at the list of professors at my father's college, and find PBroom. I am also hoping there will be time later in the day to throw basketballs into the huge trees and send the cicadas flying. So the next eight hours are completely full. A glass of water you just poured.

The Sanchez Lawn Service truck is in front of Mr. Gustafson's house again. The workers are bringing out giant trays of yellow flowers — marigolds, I think. Looks like Mr. Gustafson's house is getting a makeover, or at least a little lip gloss. I can already imagine how nice the flowers will look. I walk past the truck and make sure I spot the boy with the red cap.

"*Hola,*" I say, which is the only Spanish I know. He says it back and waves. "Those are pretty flowers. I like plants." Well, that was a genius thing to say. But he nods at me in a sweet way.

"I drank coffee today," I tell him. "It's not bad. I can see why people like it."

"*Sí,*" he says.

"And you've never done this, but I pretended to be my father last night. On the computer, I mean. I don't know why I'm telling you this."

The boy walks to the front of the house, drops to his knees, and starts making little valleys in the dirt for each plant. He waves to me as I go, and I guess we are friends now.

When I get to Charlotte's, I tell her about my investigative research, wanting to start with the Duprees, and working my way to PBroom.

"The Duprees' car hasn't moved in two days."

"So?" she says.

"So I need to know why."

"What's the second thing you need?"

"We'll need the Internet," I say.

"Ah, the type of research one does from afar."

My stomach still has a weird, floaty feeling, and I wonder if this is the coffee's fault. Tomorrow I will pour a lot of milk in it. Work my way up to the way cowboys drink it.

In Charlotte's room, I find it easy to confess how I pretended to be my father for the briefest of minutes and discovered PBroom. Her face brightens, never once judging, as if she is entertained by this fact. Then she swivels around in her chair and begins typing so quickly it makes your head spin. In not one minute, there on her computer screen is a black-and-white photo of PBroom — Patricia Broom, professor of American History, to be exact.

"What next?" she asks.

"I don't know. I just wanted to see what she looked like." Now I feel stupid for even wanting to look at her. It changed nothing. She is pretty and looks thin, if you can tell this from the neck up. There's nothing in her eyes to indicate she would hate kids. I have learned to find this expression in women. They hold an unnatural smile for too long. They force a laugh from their lips. And just as if the universe felt bad for me and wanted to reverse my mood, it gives me something else to think about. My insides give me a tight squeeze. I leave Charlotte's room. I close the bathroom door, hold my stomach. I almost want to cry and laugh at the same time.

Of course, I have an idea of what to do. I'm no oblivious Darla Jacobs. When a bunch of girls talked about it at a sleepover, she had no clue. We had to give her one.

"You know, Darla. What kind of punctuation do you put at the end of a sentence?"

"Um, a period."

"Duh."

Action is required for sure. Products needed. Maybe something special to eat. If you believe commercials, I should be out riding horses on the beach, miraculously gifted with equestrian skills. If you believe the Bible, I can be married off now, miraculously eligible just because I can bear children. I don't want to ride a horse or be married. These are things girls with mothers would know.

I want to curl into a ball, be alone, and have Charlotte with me at the same time. What is it with these opposite thoughts again? It is too much.

I can ask Charlotte to take me to CVS to get Funyuns and then, while there, I'll get products. I'll go up to the counter and pay for them both, as if I've done it all my life. Maybe throw in a pack of gum to show how casual I am.

"Sarah, you all right?" Charlotte asks through the door.

"Yeah."

"We thought we'd all go for a walk and hit those trees at the park with basketballs before it gets too hot. I told Finn you liked doing that."

Darn! How fun this would be with all *three* of us. What to do? I'll just have to be honest. After all, I am a woman now.

"Charlotte," I say, "um, I think I need your help."

She opens the door, and then I close it behind her. "I've started."

"What?"

"You know," I say, pointing south.

"Ohhhhhhhh," she says. "I thought you already had ... well, this."

I want to ask her did I already look like a woman? But this is no time. "I guess I will need something for it."

"I have a few things, and then we can run out later and get your own. We need to get you some chocolate for this, too."

Oh, this is wonderful. I almost want to cry a little and ask her to brush my hair. I feel a laugh/cry come up inside me again.

"What is it? Does it hurt? Do you feel bad?" Charlotte asks.

The strangest idea pushes its way into my head. What if this had happened when I was staying with Grandma and Gramps? Now I know something my aunt Mariah said is true in a way I cannot explain. The universe *is* listening. I thought I would have to find out all my knowledge in books, yet here is some surprise, some comfort standing right in front of me. Maybe you have to be a woman to know about the chocolate. Later, I will make a list of the new things that come with being twelve.

I tell Charlotte, "No, I feel fine."

I reach out to hug her, and we stand still a moment. Her embrace is solid, tight in a good way. I might come apart if she lets go. It's funny how you don't know you are a bunch of pieces until someone hugs you together.

We are just picking up our purses and saying bye to Finn when there he is: my father, holding a manila folder. I've seen this before when I've started a new school or gone to an after-school-care program. He pulls a background check, then makes a list of questions. If anything comes up strange, he calls his lawyer down in Houston and they gather more information on the person than even *they* knew existed. Then he sits down and has a talk with them, telling them he is to be apprised of all things concerning my welfare. Blah. Blah. Blah. I've heard it dozens of times.

"I'm taking Sarah to the store," Charlotte says.

"Is it just your brother here, then?"

I shoot a look to Finn. He has no idea about how he is about to be interrogated. He is a suspect, and my father is one of those tough cops on TV. I'm hoping there's not even a traffic ticket in that folder.

I want to shout at my dad, tell him not to embarrass me, but right now my insides are so twisty I can't. I look at him hard, letting him know the unhappy-face golf ball will appear tomorrow. *Be prepared*, I say with my mental powers. But it's no use. When my dad is wide awake, in a suit, and not drinking, there is no one more prepared, more interested in my life. I have two fathers. The drunk and the detective. This can't be normal.

Still, I'm hoping what he found will give Finn the *One-Condition Tom Nelson Seal of Approval*: one infraction in his record and it will be grandparent city for me.

chapter 21

I am in the shower, wishing the water could rise up to my neck, let me float, and be weightless. I would like to invent a machine that could take a person right out of the shower and — *poof* — they'd be dried and dressed and in bed. Skip all the boring steps in between. It would be heaven.

I've been an official woman for eight hours and officially feel tired. The only thing I like about womanness so far is my new mascara. *Swipe, swipe.* I look at least fourteen when I apply it.

Now I'm going to lie on my bed with a hot washcloth over my belly. Charlotte told me this would help the cramps in my stomach. When she took me to CVS this afternoon, she told me everything I would need to know. It was a good thing, too, because if you stand in the aisle with all those products too long, you start to feel dumb.

What I want to know is, why are there so many? She told me that I might have to try a couple of different brands to find the one just for me. All my life, I thought this would be a one-size-fits-all kind of thing, but no, it is not.

After, we went to the makeup area so Charlotte could shop for metallic eye shadow. I'm no expert on the art of these products, either, but I do like seeing all the rows of colors. Charlotte says you can pretty much put any color on your eyes. Easy. Just sweep it across and — *voilà* — you are a supermodel.

I thought of all the things I'd like to buy in the store. The colors of lipstick, for example, made me want to have one of each just for their names. Cherry Ice. Pink Sugar. China Red. Peach Crystal. I pictured myself lining them up on my bathroom counter so I could choose a different one each day. *Am I in a Pink Sugar mood today?* I could ask.

I made my way down the entire cosmetics wall and stopped at the mascara. I don't wear any makeup now, only lip gloss sometimes. Mascara seemed like something even I could do right. One or two swipes and I would have a new look. I chose Black-Brown. A present for my new status.

"Are you ready to go now?" Charlotte asked.

"Yes," I told her.

Then, pure embarrassment.

There was only a guy cashier at the front of the store. I felt my neck go red as I looked in my basket. It was so

hy I came here. The pink-and-white box practi-
med to the world, *Sarah has her period!*

Charlotte went ahead of me and bought eye shadow
for her, chocolates for me. So I looked around quickly,
added a pack of gum, a disposable camera, and a magazine to my basket. The cashier guy smiled at me, then
scanned *the* box. I made a mental note to myself: Find
out if you can order one year's supply so you don't ever
have to go through this torment. Maybe Lisa will know.
We can place a double order.

The washcloth on my belly is cold now, so I set it aside, pull
down my pajama shirt. I get out my composition notebook
(which I now hide between my mattresses) and think
about writing something for the Mr. Wistler Assignment,
see if my new woman self has something better to say than
my girl self. After all, I looked up *period* on Wikipedia. I
was relieved to find out my strange thoughts are sort of
normal if you are a real woman.

Symptoms may include fatigue, mood swings, irritability,
nervousness, confusion, depression, tearfulness, and anxiety.

Bingo. I have many of the symptoms, especially con-
fusion. For example, did I get a magazine for *me* at CVS?
No. I didn't even look to see what I was doing and grabbed
Good Housekeeping instead of *Glamour.* To make matters

worse, there is a big article in it about how to look your youngest. How will that help me?

After I look through the magazine, I am not so tired, but don't feel good, either. I feel mad, but at no one in particular.

There's a blank page in the composition book staring back at me. *What?* I want to ask it. But I am not about to start talking to a notebook. I am already talking to a plant. I send two texts to Lisa, telling her about my change and my mascara, but all she can talk about are the boys at camp and how much fun they are having swimming and making crafts out of safety pins. Well, I am just fine without her today, and I know it makes her mad that Charlotte is helping me. I don't want to make her mad, maybe a little jealous. I want someone else to feel frustrated. I am mad at so many things that don't make sense.

Normally, I don't even care that I can hear Dad's stereo playing the Beatles. Again. But right now I want to throw a basketball at the stupid thing, break it into pieces. Simon is in my thoughts today. I'm trying to work out a dream I had about him last night where he put a note in my backpack. I've had dreams of him before, but he is usually just sitting and listening to me. And I guess I am mad at my mother, too. Because of her, my grandmother is the one to buy me underwear and socks, which, *hello,*

I've outgrown and am desperate for now. But who can I tell about this? Answer: no one.

That awful sad/mad feeling washes over me again, which Charlotte keeps telling me is normal. She said I should embrace it because not everyone can hold two feelings at once, but what she doesn't know is that there is a crazy gene in me that could be causing me to feel like two different people. It feels heavy. I am a glass of water about to spill over at the slightest nudge.

I get up and head for the kitchen to get something to eat. Dad is at the stupid wobbly table as I pass by. He looks at me with a grin and starts to laugh.

"What happened to you?" he asks.

"What?"

"Around your eyes," he says. "Not sure that's the look you were going for."

I check my warped reflection in the toaster. Mascara circles both eyes and makes me look like a creature from a horror movie.

He tries to hide his laugh behind one hand, but I can tell it's still there. "I think you're supposed to wash that off, honey."

I cannot get out of the kitchen fast enough.

I slam the door to my room. I am so stupid. I don't know a lot about a lot, but I'm pretty sure a mother would not be laughing at me right now. So, I'm sorry, Lucas

McCain, *hate* might be too strong a word for my dad, but right now I'm not looking up another synonym. *Hate* will have to do.

And for my mother? I am so mad at her. You would think she could *at least* write useful things to me. Tell me about products and makeup. Something better than *Twelve is such a wonderful age.* Blah. Blah. Blah. If she thinks it's so great, she would not leave me with this humiliation.

It comes to me that there is something worse than having a mother who can't show up in a Family Tree Project. It's having a mother who doesn't show up at all. Which don't I know all about? Yes, I do.

Dear Atticus,
This letter will sound mad, but I am not mad at you. This is one of those times I could really use your advice. I flat-out don't know what to do about my father. Here I was having a good day (some interesting things happened to me today), and my dad has to be the most insensitive person on the planet. I know you've come across some insensitive people in Maycomb, and you would tell me their issues were worse than mine. That is true. But the people who are insulting people in your town (especially the way black people are treated) are ignorant, as you say. And they don't even know

the people they are calling names. So I ask you: Isn't it *worse* to be mean to someone you supposedly know and love? Well, I'm getting pretty worked up, but that's how I feel. There should be a law that forces people to follow that saying *If you can't say anything nice, don't say anything.* I tell you, that would be a good trick if you could make it happen. But then there would be a million more people in jail. You would never run out of clients. (Though I would hope you would be the prosecutor on those cases.) The guilty person (like my dad) would have to take the stand, and you could fire questions at them like, "In your opinion, Mr. Nelson, did you think it was wise to laugh at the defendant in her time of despair and hardship?"

I can hear you speaking just that way. Well, the you in the movie version of your book. I almost forgot to tell you that I watched you on TV again last night after my dad fell asleep. The picture of you I had in my mind and the one on TV are blurred together. I hope that's all right with you. By the way, you would like my new friend, Finn. He is not insensitive like some people, but is all about knowing the exact word for everything. He said that studying a word is like unpacking an old suitcase. If you want to, you can keep taking things out of the suitcase and look at them like they are brand-new. Because he knows I like fashion, he explained to me that you can match words together like an outfit of clothes and accessories. Now, I think that most people use too many accessories when they talk. You do not. You have the right amount of plainclothes words.

I especially liked the courtroom scene of the movie. Again, my smart friend Finn told me this was everybody's favorite scene, too. I like that I am ordinary that way. I wish I could have been up on that balcony with Jem and Scout to watch you work. It makes me feel like I was there. Because of the way you talk, I had to make a list of words I didn't know. Well, maybe they're not all your words. I have to remember that Harper Lee wrote you into being, but you still feel like a real, flesh-and-blood person to me. *Chifforobe* was the first one. I'd been marking up my copy of the book for a while, circling all the words I needed to look up in the dictionary. There are so many that my copy of the book will be worthless to the next person who might want to read it, so it is mine forever.

These are some words I looked up:

Umbrage

Palliation

Scuppernong

I will have to see if we have any scuppernongs around Garland. It would be nice for me to at least know I've eaten one thing you ate, too. That is weird, I know. (I hope you don't take umbrage with that. Ha-ha.)

Well, thanks for always listening to me. I already feel the tiniest bit better. (But I am still mad at my dad.)

Sincerely,
Sarah Nelson

chapter 22

When I am complaining or just saying my opinion out loud, Dad always says, "Oh, stop being so dramatic," but what does he know? From what I can see, life is super-dramatic all on its own. I'm just playing my part.

For example, this is the day the news will report another mother going to court for killing her child. It is strange to think how much can happen on a hot day in Texas, but you know, it does. Someone should investigate if the heat has anything to do with people killing each other.

I didn't know about that other mother until later, which is a good thing. I just ran out our front door and looked over at the Duprees' house. Still no movement of the long green car. I am a half hour late to Charlotte's house today. I just wanted the extra time to myself. That

p between my dad leaving and me being in some-
's company. It's a luxury. I needed it for my mood,
which is annoyed.

After my dad asked Finn about a thousand questions
until it was clear he wasn't a serial killer or an undercover
reporter, they had a friendly chat. Dad told me it mostly
centered on words and how many books they've both
read and probably how erudite they are. I can hear them
saying, *Oh, look, we are so special and erudite! Blah. Blah.
Blah.*

Erudite means "extensive knowledge from books,"
which of course I know all about because Mr. Wistler
once said he wanted to make us "erudite citizens of the
world." The trick, he said, is that you should never let
someone else hear you call yourself by that name or they
will think you are the opposite, which is ignorant. So *erudite* is a trouble word in its own way.

Charlotte's house is supercool inside and smells like
cookies. I could just take a nap.

"Try this for an hour before you succumb to TV
land," Charlotte says, handing me a copy of *The Red Badge
of Courage.* She says I will impress people if I read this
now. But I wonder if she chose this for the words *red
badge,* which if she did, it is not a funny joke.

This is a conspiracy among Dad, Charlotte, and Finn.

All three of them, with their fancy book choices. What they would think about *The Valiant Rake*, I have no idea.

I take the book from her and plop down on her sofa. I open it to the first page and already I'm bored. I could just sit here and drink Cokes and eat chips all day. Stretch out half asleep the way a dog might. Send Lisa another text message to see if she's any closer to getting a guy at camp to kiss her. Wait until I hear someone's sprinkler come on and go run through it until I am soaked. It would be a waste of time, I know. Still, it feels like a day to do something childish, something from my old self.

I hear a car door slam and run to the window. No, it is not Mr. Dupree as I'd hoped. It's Finn, walking up the sidewalk. He has on a nice plaid button-down shirt and his worn jeans that are the same blue as his eyes. I sit back down and try to arrange myself nicely, not look so lazy. My brain says to me, *So, you couldn't remember to put a little lip gloss on? What's wrong with you?*

I open the book again so Finn will be impressed.

Then, I time it just right to make my voice sound supercasual as he enters the house. "Hey."

"How's it going?"

"I was just reading." Now I know I sound real.

"I thought you only read magazines."

"Well, I don't." A whole smile takes over his face. Finn

has the kind of face you want to make smile. "So, do you have a girlfriend?"

"You get to the point, don't you?" He says this with enormous irritation. "Runs in the family."

If he only knew what else runs in the family, he would back out of the room outlaw-style, slowly and with his hands up.

"You were interrogated and found worthy," I say.

"Well, that's something, I suppose," he says. "I guess it's better to be direct."

"There's a lot of room for people to misinterpret things if you don't."

I want to tell him I come by this philosophy from moving so much. You have a short time with people, so you'd better get busy knowing them if you want a friend. Being the girl with no friends never did me any good. Plus, girls with no friends get picked on by Darts.

"So? A girlfriend?"

"Not at the moment," he says, which makes my heart smile. "What are you reading?" He lifts the cover of the book. "Good one."

"I should be more into it, but it's so hot," I tell him. "Why does the heat make you want to do nothing?"

"Summer should be lazy," he says. I wonder if he can read my mind because that was my exact thought.

He pulls a book from his backpack. I can't tell what it

is, but it's superthick and green, so it must be a textbook. Those kinds of books aren't just good for reading. They can also prop up the jack under your car when you need to change your tire, which is what my dad did once when we had a flat.

"I have another question," I say.

"Shocking," he says, all dramatic.

"When did you take my iPod to put those two songs on it?"

"When you and Charlotte were doing some top secret girl stuff." Then he says, "And by the way, you're welcome."

"What's up with that?"

"I found your song list deficient," he says.

"It's what I like."

"You don't have to listen to what people think a twelve-year-old should like, you know," he says. I can't give him the satisfaction of knowing I liked his song choices a little. I only listened to them five times.

I read for what feels like a million and a half years, but is really just thirty minutes. The sprinklers at Mr. Gustafson's go on and off. The dog that lives inside the chain-link fence of Mr. Stanley's yard barks and barks and barks at nothing. Someone outside the cul-de-sac bounces a basketball. I can't concentrate on the page with all the unstoppable life going on outside. I wish I were standing on the tree stump. But then I wouldn't want to waste time

I have with Finn. If I end up having to lie about my first kiss, I've decided Finn is in the top two for my selection.

"Want to watch TV?" I ask. "We'll keep it low so it won't bother Charlotte. And I promise I'll read more later."

"Fine by me."

I flip on the TV, but it takes minutes to warm up. You've never seen such an ancient contraption as this. It's a giant wooden box holding a TV hostage inside it.

"Suggestions," I ask, afraid I'll select a show that screams *I am a twelve-year-old*. What I'd like to watch is *The Price Is Right*, although I am better at *Jeopardy!*

"How about *The Price Is Right*?" and there it is. We have another thing in common.

Drew Carey bounces across the stage clapping and greeting the lucky contestants who want more than anything to win matching washer-dryer sets, a trampoline, or a chandelier. These are the easy items to guess at, but wait until they start bringing in huge cars or vacation trips. Those can be tricky. My dad is the all-time winner of those guesses at our house — how does he know, if he never goes anywhere?

A woman leaps up and down after correctly guessing the price of a laptop computer. Big deal. Everyone knows that. The show pauses for a commercial. A short newsbreak comes into the programming, letting you know the top headlines. They always do this in the mornings so lazybones people watching game shows can have at least some idea of what's going on in the world.

I move to get off the sofa and go to the bathroom when the announcer, a pretty woman in a red suit, stops me flat.

"This is only the second time in Texas's history the charge has been brought forth, the first time being the case of Thomas Nelson following the trial of his wife, Jane Nelson." And there she is, entering my life unannounced and unwanted. A picture of my mother in a white shirt, a pale blue wall in the background, the kind they use to take school pictures of first graders. I've never seen this photo before.

"I have to go now."

Finn might have said something to me, but all my senses are turned off. I think this is what they call numb.

I picture my too-pink room, see myself putting my things in moving boxes, hear the squeaky stretch of packing tape as it unrolls and hugs the sides of a box that will move to our fifth different address. Picking up Plant and telling her she'll have a new window. We will have to patch the holes in my dad's closet, make sure the kitchen cabinets are empty.

There are so many things to think about. I will become *that* girl. Again.

Finn clicks the TV off. I see my reflection in the screen. I look much farther away than I really am.

I close my eyes so I won't have to look at myself, and I hear the voice of that mean girl saying, "Oh, are you *that* girl?" Something about the way she leaned into the word *that* pulled me to a dead stop in the hallway. There's something about age nine that perks up a person's nosiness. Nosy girls came into my world, and they were named Gina Graham.

Gina Graham had a locker right next to mine. Hers was decorated so much with *G-I-N-A*, you would think she had a hard time remembering her name. I had already had an idea about girls like Gina. They are the ones with naturally loooooong blond hair. They dominate the playground. They announce to the world they have a boyfriend, even if you couldn't care less. They are only children. They don't smile. They intimidate you. They are Darts.

"My mother told me you are the girl whose mother went crazy," Gina said. I just slammed my locker shut and let my feet do the talking. But she wouldn't quit the idea. She raced to stand right in front of me, put her superblond head right in my path, and said, "Are you crazy, too?"

I said the most intelligent thing I could think of. "Shut up! You don't know what you're talking about," I continued, feeling a rise of tears in the back of my eyes. Somehow my body knew I wasn't going to win.

"Yes, I do. You're that girl," she barked.

I took myself to the bathroom to hide. I had a long private cry and tried to think of ways I could disappear, dissolve into the cracks in the tile floor. Then I thought that Gina would be walking on me, so that was no good.

I sat there through the next class, replaying Gina's cold words.

Sarah has a crazy mother.

Before the principal came to find me, I'd written lies about Gina on the bathroom wall. I did it with my left hand so it would look like a maniac's writing.

How I came to be standing in the middle of our cul-de-sac, I have no idea. I would love to see the instant replay. Did I walk or run? I don't know. What I do know is that I've all of a sudden figured out my dream about Simon. He was trying to warn me by putting that note in my backpack. It's a sure sign of crazy that I believe in dreams about my brother, but I do. Somebody call the hospital and let them take me now, but I know Simon is still connected to me in a way I cannot describe. There's no word in the dictionary for it but *twin*.

Finn followed me out here, too, and we are just standing in the heat, saying nothing. It is so hot. The smell of the wastewater-treatment plant is already sharp. I hold my breath, and the cramps in my stomach come in waves.

I have to keep moving or my brain will create a horror movie called *Everyone Knows My Business.*

"There will be a U-Haul in front of our house," I tell Finn. There is Dad carrying a box with the word *fragile* written in black marker. There is the new place, a pile of crumpled newspaper at my feet in the kitchen as I decide if the glasses should be near the sink or the dishwasher. There is our mail, each piece covered with a yellow forwarding-address label on it.

"Why do you think you'll move?"

"We always do."

There's a stone inside my flip-flop so I kick my shoe off and feel the heat from the pavement come up through my foot. I regard the house I live in now, try to see it as it was when we got here on the first day.

"Did you know who lived here before us?"

"No."

"You can always pick them out, you know. Rent-houses."

"How?"

"It's like seeing someone wearing fashion from ten years ago. You know. And there's always the bad grass."

"I guess a tree stump is a giveaway, too."

"Yeah, no one would have a stump on purpose, would they?"

I climb up on the stump and feel the tiniest breeze on my face.

"My mother isn't dead," I tell him, tears coming now. He walks around and faces me. "She's just crazy, or if you don't care for that word, terminally unreachable."

"I'm sorry."

"My family is strange," I say.

"Strange. Unusual. Peculiar. Odd," he says. "Sorry, can't help it. Hey, I'll delete those songs if you want."

"No, they can stay," I say, and then, "Please don't tell anyone." But I realize how stupid my request is. The world knows. Aliens from other planets know.

"Tell anyone what?" he says, and I look at his face just as he is winking at me. I catch it in my heart, know I'll take it out later to look at.

"I don't want to go back inside," I tell him. "It's like the TV knows."

"That TV is so old, it has a bad memory. It will forget by the time *Jeopardy!* comes on."

Don't ask me how I know this, but I think he could be the security guard outside the vault of secrets. Sorry, Jimmy. Finn is now number one on my list of potential boyfriends. He would never tell.

chapter 23

If I am forced to do the seventh-grade Family Tree Project, the world will know what I already know to be true. The crazy gene is taking root, setting up a town inside me. Streets near my lungs. A park near my heart. Roller coasters around my skull. But since we will probably move, I guess Problem 2 of my summer is now solved. That's the thing about problems. One gets solved, and there is a new one ready to take its place.

Now, the only thing to keep from thinking about it is to keep moving. I leap from the stump.

"Where are you going?" Finn asks.

"To get an answer," I say.

The Duprees' front door is a nice shade of cocoa brown. My fist pounds on the front door. Then I realize I should be softer. *Tap. Tap. Tap.* I ring the doorbell and hear its chiming sound within. Still no answer. None. It is silent and it makes me angry. Why isn't anyone answering?

Then, a shift in the curtains at the window followed by the click of the door unlocking.

"Yes," Mrs. Dupree says, opening the door, her eyes squinting. "Can I help you?"

"Hello," I say, unsure and shaky. "Your car hasn't moved. I was worried."

Her face folds in on itself, and she grabs the fabric of her housedress. It is then I notice she is not put together in any way. She is completely undone. Hair, face, and dress are all of someone who has been sleeping for a long time.

"Sarah," she manages. "Oh, my dear, sorry to have worried you, but..." Her voice trails off, and her eyes land on the ground. If she could finish the sentence, you just know that the last word would be heartache or one of its synonyms.

"Can we help you?" I ask. She looks up, and I can tell this is the first time she has noticed Finn. "This is my friend Finn. He's a linguistics student and not in any way dangerous." I say this like I'm the lead investigator and that is Finn's credential.

"Mr. Dupree," she says. Then her body shivers and says what her mouth can't speak. Something bad has happened. I knew it.

She motions for us to come inside. The three of us

stand in her entryway. Finn and I wait for her to keep moving, but she doesn't. Against one wall are a giant mirror and an empty coatrack. I watch Mrs. Dupree's reflection, waiting for what to do next. Right now this small space is the loneliest place on earth.

"Let's go sit down, children, and I'll tell you about Mr. Dupree."

I've seen enough daytime talk shows to know there isn't much you can say to a grieving person. No amount of telling them *Hey, I know what you're going through, it will get better, and time heals all wounds* will help. But for some reason, people still hang on to these sentences like emotional life preservers. Someone should toss them in the trash. They are worn out. I don't say anything, let Mrs. Dupree talk.

"I don't want you to feel low because of my loss," she says. "I just wish Mr. Dupree was here, you know."

Then her tears overcome her face and there is quietness for a long, long time. I know about loss, I could say, even though I know it wouldn't help. I have felt low already, so anything you say will only make me nod and think, yes, I know. I lost someone, too. We could form a club.

For example, I wonder at all the ways me and Simon would be alike. I guess at the things he'd enjoy, so I can do them instead since he didn't get the chance, like when I was on a soccer team.

There are a few pictures of the two of us I stare at. I don't know how, but someday I will take one of his pictures to a crime lab. Let them do that age-progression thing like they do for junk-mail-envelope missing children so you can see what they'd look like today. Wouldn't I love to see what Simon would look like at twelve? Yes, I would.

Mrs. Dupree's face is wet now with more tears, and she just lets them fall right onto the plastic mat on her kitchen table, then runs her finger through a puddle of them as she explains about her husband's death. Pretty soon, Mrs. Dupree has memories to spare of the man she spent more than forty years with. And she doesn't mind sharing them right here and now. She is a book determined to be read.

"Not only could he do wonderful woodworking projects," she goes on, "but he could make pens. Did I tell you that? He made pens out of fine pink wood, and he would give them as presents for Christmas."

"I didn't even know there was such a thing as pink wood," I say.

"Are you sure you don't want another apple, dear?" she asks, touching the top of my hand with hers. The difference in our two hands is like fire and ice. She has lived the life of someone who has worked hard, and my hands have done nothing. She's traveled, and I've stayed home all my life. I hope my hands are like hers someday. Mapped and interesting.

"No, thanks," I say.

"What about your friend? Would you like more, young man?" she asks.

"No. Thanks."

The kitchen fills up with words not being said. They float about us. Bubble thoughts waiting to be assigned to a head. I am used to having questions I can't ask from living with my father. Only now, it feels good to be silent. My grandmother would say we are bathing in the silence. I like that idea. I pretend we are washing off the misery of Mrs. Dupree's grief and reporters interrupting *The Price Is Right* with bad news. We sit there and listen to the apple wall clock tick, tick, tick.

After a thousand ticks, Finn says, "Mrs. Dupree, is there anything I can do for you around the house? Do you need something moved, fixed?" The way Finn ends his sentence is so full of help.

"Oh, aren't you a dear. My son is coming this weekend," Mrs. Dupree says. "There's not much to do. It all just happened. I rolled over and he was gone. And then, you just call the authorities and they take him away. Our arrangements had all been made years ago. All I have to do is decide what to wear. It should be harder than that, don't you think? To take care of someone who has died? There should be more." She is weeping again, so I take hold of her hand. It's all I can think to do.

"I lost my father a few years back," Finn says, "and it was hard." I kick him under the table for saying the exact wrong thing, comparing one death to another.

"I'm sorry for your loss," she says.

Finn gives me a scolded-dog look so I know he gets my meaning.

I scan the dim house for family pictures. The best way to have a friend is to ask them about themselves. A picture might give me a good starting point. Mrs. Dupree pulls her hand away from me and begins smoothing out the place mat, which is already smooth as can be. I notice a beautiful diamond band across her ring finger. It looks like it was just born. Shiny and new.

"Is that your wedding ring?" I ask.

She regards her hands, looking at them as if she is just this minute aware they are attached to her. "Oh my, this? Yes, dear." She slides it off then, easy as you please, and extends it to me.

She explains how there is a pattern of three diamonds, a ruby, three diamonds, a ruby. How Mr. Dupree wanted rubies because she looked so pretty in red. And diamonds, of course, because he thought she was sparkling. A thin silver band was all he could afford when they were first wed, and then he gave her ten roses on their tenth wedding anniversary, handing them to her one at a time, the last rose bearing the new ring. It's about the sweetest thing I've ever heard.

"Would you two care for another apple?" she asks again. Well, this time it just wouldn't be polite to say no. And instead of silence, the three of us listen to the sharp, crisp sound of three people eating apples. We sit this way until Charlotte's voice can be heard shouting out in the cul-de-sac. I get to Mrs. Dupree's window fast and see her standing in the center of the street, screaming my name. Well, if that isn't embarrassing. Finn and I step outside and wave to her.

"We're over here with Mrs. Dupree," I tell her.

"I can't believe you guys just left," she says angrily. "Your father is not paying me enough to worry about where you disappeared to." She says more about me needing to call him right away and what were you thinking, Finn, taking her out without even leaving a note?

There is more to listen to, I am sure, but all I can picture is my father handing Charlotte ten-dollar bills to babysit me. I didn't know about this. I am so stupid sometimes.

chapter 24

When I was younger, I wanted to be an astronaut. This wasn't because I had any special knowledge about space, which I didn't. It was because I wanted to see the whole Earth all at once. I saw pictures in a book of what it looked like from space and wanted to see it for myself. A marbled swirl of blue and white. Then I heard an astronaut say he could put his hand up to the space shuttle window and hide a big chunk of the planet behind it. You have to wonder if God does that once in a while just because He can. He might even want to hide certain people just to see what things look like on Earth without them.

Tonight, I would blot out Charlotte and my dad. My dad still thinks I need a babysitter. And I can't believe she is getting paid to be with me. It is a deep pain I didn't expect. She is an accessory to the crime.

accessory *n*.: a person who incites someone to commit a crime or assists the perpetrator of a crime, either before or during its commission

Dad got home from work early. I thought we would talk about the news story, make some kind of plan. I would let it slide that I knew about his undercover babysitting plot. But when he came into the house and put his briefcase on the kitchen counter, he just kissed my head and said, "Let's not talk about this now."

Of course that's what he'd say.

"Did PBroom find out? Did she see the news?" I asked him.

"I have no idea," he said. "We'll just wait and see." *Wait and see* means stop talking about this, Sarah, and change the subject.

"We went to check on Mrs. Dupree and found out about her dead husband," I said. "It's very sad."

"He was a nice man," Dad replies.

Dad tried to pretend life was normal, like there weren't a thousand and one things to talk about. He'd finally remembered to bring home pork chops, which turned out awful because we have the worst kitchen stove in the history of kitchen stoves. The top is slanted to the left side, so you have to pay attention all the time and turn your food around constantly. The oil slides to one side and the meat gets browned there, black on the other side if you aren't watching it, which is what happened to me. We had to eat half-brown, half-burned pork chops.

After dinner, I attempted to get another conversation going.

"Do you think a reporter will call us?"

"You don't need to worry about this."

"There are things I need to know, like are we going to move?" I asked.

"I don't know."

He went into his office like he always does and closed the door.

I sat outside and eavesdropped while he called Grandma and Gramps. There wasn't much I could write in my notebook, just a lot of *Mmm-hmmm*s. Maybe he is getting so much better it doesn't bother him. No, that is probably not it. The less he talks, the more bothered he is.

So the way I see it, I was in my right to do what I did. There are ways to make a person talk.

I have ways.

First, I went to the garage, took his Jim Beam bottle and started to pour it into Plant. Then I realized I was killing her, which just shows how stupid I am. I apologized to her and then emptied the bottle in the toilet. *Flush!* It is gone.

Then I refilled his bottle with apple juice. Ha! I can't wait until he finds it all missing. We'll see how he feels about things getting switched on him without his knowledge. Still, I worry about getting Plant drunk. I am going to stay up all night with her, make sure she is all right. If her leaves are droopy tomorrow, I will Google what to do.

Now my room feels too hot to sleep. My mind is still running in different directions. I hug my blanket to my chest, try to get it to hug me back, but then I am too hot and kick the sheets off. I turn my pillow over, hold on to the cool side, press it against my skin, and try to stop thinking about how every person in Garland knows our secret. Jimmy Leighton and even Mr. Wistler. I cram my head into the pillow, but it is no use.

So I think of the only thing I can do now. I pop out the window screen, slip into the yard, taking Plant with me. A sliver of light from the full moon stripes the yard, and I follow it outside. It's warm out, but the air smells sharp, like newly cut grass, and I think, *Why don't I ever sleep outside?*

I place Plant on the grass and lie down in the front yard, stretching out into a summer snow angel. The sky is clear and open. Time to switch off the mind like a light. Mine is the only one still on, still running in a loop. A dog barks a couple of blocks over. I like his sound. Even and sure. It's constant and doesn't change, almost like a recording.

I wonder if Dad would let me get a dog. A medium-sized one would be fine. Not so big as to knock you down when you come home. A furry little thing to tell all my secrets to. But then, there are no real secrets. Not when the biggest thing can interrupt *The Price Is Right* and expose you in front of a linguistics student. There is no magazine article on the planet with advice on this particular kind of catastrophe.

A small clicking sound interrupts my thoughts. I think it's a bird, but no, it is a man in front of Charlotte's house. I can tell it's you-know-who by the way his shoulders are sloped forward and the *clomp, clomp, clomp* of his stupid boots. I wonder why I didn't hear his car drive up. He's throwing something at the window, reaching into his pockets and doing it again and again. Her light finally comes on. I flatten myself out in the grass so he won't see me. Charlotte slides her window up. It is so quiet I can hear their whispery voices. It's like I'm on a stakeout, gathering evidence.

"What are you doing?"

"You told me to come over and to be quiet."

"You couldn't use the front door?"

"I thought it might wake someone up."

"My mother is gone, remember?"

She says come to the front door like a normal person, and he does.

The porch light flashes on, and she slips out onto the steps. They sit on the front step, and he puts his arm around her.

"I wanted to talk about…" she says, but then stops in the middle of her sentence, leaving the mystery hanging there.

I am still and frozen, desperate to know what they are talking about now. But they are not talking. The sounds coming from her porch are of gum smacking, but would they be chewing gum now? I wish I could watch this up close, see how it's done. Just hearing the noises without seeing the action is gross.

"No, stop it. Stop it," I hear Charlotte say.

"Come on," he says. "Come on."

I don't hear Christopher say anything. I lift my head slightly just in time to see him on top of her.

"Christopher!" she says. "No, not now."

The tone of her voice lets me know she's in trouble. I wonder if I should do anything, call out. What would investigators do now? They certainly wouldn't stay pinned to the grass, but here I am. I felt this same way when I was a kid and thought a monster was under my bed, waiting to grab my ankle and pull me under the mattress. My strategy then, as now, was to stay as still and mute as possible. I decide that I will count to twenty and then get up. I will make myself move.

Then, I hear more of her shouts. A loud thump as if someone has fallen to the porch.

I hear the door slam. Then, Finn's even voice. "Go

174

home." If I were Christopher, I would be afraid of Finn. But Christopher curses at him, then calls Charlotte a tease and a couple of other words. I turn my head a little. I hear Christopher's boots clomp down the sidewalk. There is a car door slam. He does a 180 turn in the middle of the cul-de-sac, and headlights spray across our lawn. I pray he keeps going and doesn't spot me.

Charlotte's crying and shouting something completely unintelligible at Christopher's moving car. Whatever she says makes Christopher's car stop, change gears, and move in reverse.

"You're going to regret that!" he shouts. His voice is clear as glass.

"Get out of here!" Finn shouts.

The sound of something hard crashing against metal rings out, and Christopher's car zooms away. I prop myself up on my elbows and catch Finn beaning rocks into Christopher's car fender.

I wish I could see Charlotte's expression. There is so much more being said in her eyes than any words would say. She goes inside and Finn stands alone on the sidewalk. There is a moon shadow of his body on the ground. I screw up my courage and do my best to whisper and shout at once.

"Finn!"

"Sarah?"

"Over here." I've broken my cover, but it is okay.

He turns and walks toward me.

"What happened?" I ask him.

"What are you doing out here?"

"Staring at the moon and wishing I was there."

He sits down on the grass next to me. I lie back and so does he.

"You can blot out the entire moon with one thumb." I show him how it's done, and he does it, too. "And from a distance, you can blot out an entire person."

"Is that wishful thinking, too?"

I give him a smile as my answer even though he can't see it in the dark. The cool night air washes over us, and suddenly Garland doesn't seem like a dull, drab town where nothing interesting ever happens.

"Sarah!"

Dad's voice is filled with anger. His breath probably smells of apple juice. Ha-ha! I picture his puzzled face as he realizes he'd been tricked.

I hide the moon behind my thumb. If I could be on the moon and blot out the entire world, I would.

Dad shouts, "Sarah, where are you?"

Finn asks, "Are you going to answer him?"

"I hate him. He drinks too much because of her. He's so immature."

"*Sarah!*"

"Plus, I can't hear him because I'm pretending to be in

space." And we lie there looking at the stars. Finn's phone goes off. That beep that tells you a message is incoming. He looks at it, stuffs it back in his pocket. I hope my father didn't hear it.

"Who is that?"

"This girl."

"And?"

"And what?"

"You like her?"

"I guess. She's smart."

Ha! I can be smart, too.

His phone goes off again, but this time he turns it off.

"Sarah! You better answer me!"

"Should you go in?" Finn wants to know.

"I still can't hear him," I say. "You can't hear sound in space like we do on Earth. Sound needs something to travel in, like a gas or solid."

"Well, thanks for the info."

I am impressed with myself. "Science fair. Third place." There it is, proof of my smartness on a shiny white ribbon.

"So how can you hear me?"

"You are in space, too." But not with that girl and her texts. She must stay on Earth and become stupid while we discover a new galaxy. I will let Finn name it even though it is clear I know more about space than him.

"Fine, stay in your room, then," my dad calls out.

Fine. I will.

The sky twinkles with dark blue possibility. Diamonds against velvet. Finn rests comfortably next to me as if he wants to be here. My mind records the whole scene, tucks it away safely so I can play the night again and again.

chapter 25

In the morning, the ceiling fan whirls above me, making a rickety beat that sounds like *you're-going-to-get-it, you're-going-to-get-it*. I turn it off and open the window to the hot, hot air. I don't want to shut it. I need more room to breathe or possibly a quick way to escape. For all I know, I will be in this pink jail for the rest of my life. He will be angry with me. He'll have that silent kind of anger, which is the worst. There is no way to enter a person's mind when he is silent. And of course, it will be my fault. I knew *drunk* was a trouble word.

When I came inside last night, we'd stood in the narrow hallway, me on one end, him on the other, holding the empty bottle of Jim Beam like we were in a showdown, guns ready to draw.

"What were you doing outside?" he asked. "Why didn't you come when I called you?"

I used my right to remain silent and waited to hear the smash of glass, see the shatter of a thousand pieces against the wall. There was already a place in the wall that someone else had patched and painted over.

He said, "Is there something you want to tell me?"

"No."

"Are you sure?"

"I think my actions pretty well covered it."

"Don't get smart with me, Sarah!"

"Then don't get drunk on me, Dad!"

It was like some other girl in Garland said those words, not me. I am not that brave. But this other girl who looks like me, well, she had courage. She could speak trouble words, no problem.

After what felt like a hundred years, he walked toward me, held me close. The opposite of what you'd expect in a showdown. I could smell the cologne I gave him last Father's Day, a brand I'd discovered in one of those magazine inserts offering a strip of scent. When the hug was over, he held me at arm's length, his eyes to the floor. Then he said good night and walked back into his room and closed the door. I heard him get up this morning, run the shower, raise the cranky garage door, and drive away without a word. I know from experience that Dad's delayed punishments are his worst punishments, which means I'll have an entire day to suffer.

All I can do this morning is try to figure out what happened between Charlotte and Christopher. When I sent her a text message this morning, her reply was that she didn't feel well. I asked her if Christopher was coming over, which I was sure he wasn't. She only replied love is difficult. Nothing I heard last night sounded like anything having to do with love. But then, what do I know about love and relationships? Answer: nothing.

I was seven when my father divorced my mother.

He told me in his gentle voice he'd try to make her life as soft as possible. The word stuck to the roof of my mouth. A *soft life*. I suppose it was the right word. *Soft*.

soft *adj.*: smooth and agreeable to the touch; not rough or coarse

"I should have done it a long time ago," he said.

When he took the papers to her at the hospital, I watched them from a distance. I am remembering more now, putting the puzzle pieces about my mother on paper in my notebook. This was my second visit to the hospital. We sat outside. I read a book while he walked over and talked to her.

When I looked up from my book, I thought, *There is a nice couple talking*. It would have made a nice painting. But then, you could see her folding into herself a bit, her hands sitting in her lap, playing with some piece of paper, folding and refolding it again and again. Her doctor told us she'd taken an origami class, which sounded strange to me because why would you have to take a class to fold a piece of paper? Later, he would show us the paper birds and butterflies she'd made, each of them creased by her own hand. Tens and tens of them on her nightstand, her windowsill, arranged artfully around her dressing table. I stole two of them, hid them between the pages of my book.

While Dad talked, her fingers worked as if they'd memorized the twists and turns, knew exactly how to command the paper so it would yield to a shape. At one point, her face turned toward the sky and you knew that was the moment he said the word *divorce*, a trouble word if there ever was one.

Dad wore his wedding ring right up until the day the divorce was final. I know because I asked him that day if I could have it. He slid it off right away, put it in my palm, and went into his room to get drunk on Jim Beam. He wasn't supposed to do this, of course. I heard my grandmother tell him not to, her voice so loud on the phone you could make out every syllable. But he ignored her, and I didn't see why it was a bad thing to do the day you break up with someone. I just hoped it would be the last breakup I would ever see.

I keep the origami birds and his gold wedding band in my box of important stuff, including the letters and newspaper clippings about my mother's trial and then his trial, too. I'm not sure why it was important for me to have it, but it seemed wrong to toss it out, which was what he'd said he was going to do with it. I figured you should keep something that once made you happy. His sad feelings wouldn't last forever, I thought.

But like I said, what do I know about relationships?

chapter 26

Here is another thing you have to learn on your own: You can make all kinds of plans, but if you are twelve and don't have a car, you might as well forget about them. You are at the mercy of someone with a driver's license. Still, this is what I'm doing right now, making plans, even though Plant agrees it's futile, which is my new favorite word.

futile *adj.*: incapable of producing any result; ineffective; useless; not successful

Sometimes you meet a new word and think, where have you been all my life? *Futile* is such a word. Many things I've done have been futile. Like today I'm making lists of my options when we move. Practicing writing my name with a fancy *R* as my middle initial is one way to throw people off the track that I am Jane Nelson's daughter. Also, I'm considering going by Rose. Rose Nelson seems like the name of an old woman who wears a hat to church, though. I've seen them at my grandparents' church. Maybe there are other options. Ways to disguise myself.

Now that Garland knows my secret, I am also packing my bag to leave. After talking it over with Plant, we agree that a good strategy is to move away to avoid nosy reporters and mean Darts. My plan is to go to Aunt Mariah's house, which is not exactly running away from Dad. It is running toward another family member. Even Scout and Jem had their aunt Alexandra to help them while Atticus worked. That will be my logical argument when my disappearance is discovered.

Oh, I was just going to visit family, which is not dangerous at all and really makes life easier for you, Dad. You may send my mail here, please.

A bonus to this plan is that it solves Problem 2, which is back in a big way. I figure I will go to seventh grade in Aunt Mariah's town, where there is no Family History Project to make me miserable.

If not for the computer, I would be lost, but no, I am not. I have the Greyhound bus schedule and her address, which I've written in my real diary. When I arrive, she will surely help me. I know I will be in trouble with my father, but I think it's better to have the information first and be in trouble later. I've heard my father say more than once to Grandma, "You know what they say, 'Better to ask forgiveness later than permission first.'" When he says this, she rolls her eyes like he's said the most irritating words ever.

"Why must you be so stubborn, Tom," she had asked the last time. "It was a good job and you just left it. Good teaching jobs like that don't come along every day."

"It's my choice."

"You are in your own little world. Making your life into a box."

"I'm protecting what I still have."

"Don't think I don't know you still drink far too much."

Chop. Chop. Chop. More carrots into a pile for her.

"Well, sorry to disappoint you."

Click. Click. Click. More ice cubes in a glass for him.

You don't have to be the Queen of Obvious to see he's not crazy about his mother and her opinions. This would make you wonder why he's always thought it was a good idea to send me to her house every summer. And also, she drinks her wine, too, so can you really tell someone not to drink if you have one in your own hand?

These are questions I leave in my fake diary just in case he snoops around my room. Did my dad have parents

186

who didn't answer his questions? If so, what did he do? That is how much I want to solve the mystery of their relationship. But I will do that at a distance now. That is called getting objective evidence, which I will have plenty of time to do when I'm gone.

While I am busy making plans and breakfast, I hear a knock on the door. It's Finn, informing me Charlotte is taking the day off so I'm stuck with him. My stomach does a flip because I don't consider being with him stuck at all.

"What's wrong with her?" I ask. I want to know if he'll tell me the parts I did not see when I spied on them on their lawn.

"She had a big fight with what's-his-face. I don't think we'll be seeing him again," he says. "Good riddance." Of course, I'll believe this when I see it. Lisa told me the first breakup never takes. For some reason, you have to go through it twice for it to stick.

"Well, my grandma always said you should have two boxes marked Goodwill and Good Riddance." I wonder how it's possible I can sound so uncool. It is because of the bad news. But he smiles anyway. I made him smile.

"Anyway, we do have a job today," he says. "Wouldn't want to be a slacker. Mrs. Dupree needs help packing her books. She said we could have any of the books we wanted and she'd donate the rest."

He hands me a small hardbound book. "I got this one for you already."

You will not believe it, but it's *To Kill a Mockingbird* by Harper Lee. A real hardback copy, too.

I open the book with care, run a hand over the title page, and take in the old-book smell, which is practically indescribable. The next page has handwriting. I don't know why, but seeing the signature kind of takes my breath away, too, makes her seem real, which, of course, she is. I want to touch it the way I touch my mother's writing, see if I can picture her holding the pen as she wrote it there.

With my love,
Nelle Harper Lee

"Mr. Dupree actually met her once," Finn says.

I am careful with the book, let the pages fall where they want to go. It opens to a page with a sticky note. This is what I read:

"Our mother died when I was two," says Scout, "so I never felt her absence."

"I thought this was poignant," he says. "I thought it would help."

"With what?" I ask.

"The Price Is Right."

"Oh."

"It was a stupid idea," he says.

"No, not stupid," I say. "Thanks." I put a note in my head to look up *poignant* in the dictionary.

My mind swirls and I feel suddenly shy. I am not strong like Scout. I feel my mother's absence all the time. More and more as I get older. Maybe if I had a brother like Jem, a father like Atticus. Maybe then I would be like Scout.

It is strange how I share this secret with Finn. Strange he would give me a gift of words. I try to remember what I know about boys. Last summer I read a magazine article called *Six Secrets He Won't Tell You*. I cut them out and used the page as a bookmark until I'd memorized the list.

1. He liked you much earlier than he let on.
2. He likes long walks on the beach.
3. He does like to cuddle.
4. He'd rather not go to your mother's for dinner.
5. He believes he's the only one you've ever been with (or would prefer to think of it that way).
6. His actions will always reveal more than his words.

I shared the article with Lisa, too. We dissected each secret for clues. She'd said, Well, why would he want to have dinner with my mom in the first place? She had a point.

Now, I look from the book to Finn's face. I am smart enough to know I shouldn't say anything but thank you very much. And I do. There is a new way he looks at me when I say it, and I wonder if he sees what I feel.

"Anyway, we all have big secrets," he says.

"Really? What's yours?" I ask. "Do you have a tattoo somewhere?"

He leans into the door frame, studies his shoes.

"My dad killed himself when I was eleven."

Then, time waits for him to speak again. That's how big the secret is. It has to come out slow. "Apparently, I look just like him, which is a real problem for my mother," he says. "She still has a big reminder of him, you know, whether she wants it or not. So when he died, I sort of lost both my parents, you know. I was mad at both of them, but that doesn't help. I think that's how it might be with your dad."

I swallow hard. This is the kind of information you want to run and be alone with, dissect it and break it down to be sure you heard it right.

"It sucks" is all I can say.

"I agree with your choice of verb," he says.

"At least your secret cannot be announced during *The Price Is Right*."

"Touché."

It comes to me there's a heavy feeling on my chest and lightness in my stomach all at once. I can't be sure, but I think love is someone who gets you. And I think that someone is standing in front of me.

"Ice cream. We should eat ice cream," I say.

"Definitely."

Even though I've barely eaten breakfast, I make us two huge bowls of Fudge Ripple, and we sit on our front step, eating and talking about books. Then, we pack up a hundred of Mrs. Dupree's books, and it takes forever because we have to look at them all. It is the best day of my life.

Dear Atticus,

There is trouble in Garland. I wish it was the kind of trouble a lawyer like you could help with. Do you know how many lawyers have commercials now, shouting from your TV screen about deserving justice and getting the most money right into your pocket? Well, these things do exist. I don't like those commercials one bit, and I can tell you—**you** would never be a lawyer like that. I would love to throw one hundred copies of your book at their faces. You would never need to have a commercial. If there was a crime of injustice or something, you would have words to help me solve my problem.

You would tell me my actions have little to do with how I feel and most to do with what is right. There is no clear right in this situation. It would be helpful to have Scout or Jem with me now. They would know what life looks like from my height, which is what I need most. Someone to really look at things from where I stand. Why can't you be my father? Well, enough of that, you would say.

So here is what I can tell you. There was a news story about my mother on TV. Why people must pull out this old dusty story, I have no idea. I don't think it adds anything to the other stories about other mothers, but someone at the buildings where news is created thinks so. Since I don't know what my dad is planning to do about this, I am thinking up what to do on my own. It is simple, really. I'm going to go live with my aunt for a while. If it goes well, maybe I'll stay there forever. It would be good to live with a woman. I know you understand because you let your sister, Alexandra, come help out with Scout and Jem. Actually, I got the idea of staying with my aunt from your book. No offense to you, but sometimes I don't think Scout knows how good she has it, having a woman help her become a proper lady. I wish I could talk to my dad about this, Atticus, get him to see things my way, which he plain never will.

Sincerely,
Sarah Nelson

P.S. A person said the other day that a porch is not really Southern unless it has ferns on it. Do you think this is so? Should I go to Alabama to see for myself? I hope this is true. I get along very well with plants.

chapter 27

Dad is spending all his time in the office, door shut and locked. I hear typing and low conversations, but without the courage to pick up the other phone to hear the other voice, I don't know what is happening. He is making plans, and so am I. We haven't talked about it, but I feel it coming. Something big. I am afraid to tell Plant we are leaving again, one way or another. She's getting used to the window in my room. Except for the one night with Jim Beam, Garland has been good to her. Well, she's heard me despair about the seventh-grade Family Tree Project, so I know she'll understand.

And another strange occurrence is that I found PBroom listed on our caller ID. This has never happened before, so I can't decide which box this goes in. Good or bad.

I've decided I cannot move to Aunt Mariah's until

after the funeral. If there is one thing I want them to say about me after I've gone, it is this: Wasn't it nice of her to stay until Mr. Dupree was buried? Plus, Mrs. Dupree invited me to help her make apple pies today and it would look suspicious if I refused. I left my dad a note and walked across the cul-de-sac. The hot concrete was already sizzling and made me want to crack an egg and watch it fry.

Inside Mrs. Dupree's house are a thousand sweet smells: vanilla, coffee, cinnamon, apples, and cloves. Her son is so lucky. I bet he had delicious food in his lunch every day, a plate of warm cookies always on the table. I know she loves him that much. There are pictures of her family everywhere, the walls so full of frames that I don't know what color the inside of her house really is. And the frames on the mantel are placed just the way I would do it. Straight ahead so you have to stop and look.

I watch her rolling out the pie dough under her papery fingers with an amazing strength. She is stronger than you would suspect for an old woman. I want to be honest with her, ask her if she'll teach me, gift me with useful cooking knowledge before it's too late and the only recipe I can teach someone is Hamburger Helper, which is no recipe at all. If Dad was a fan of the cooking channel instead of Westerns, maybe I'd know more about cooking than playing poker.

Now, I must know how to bake an apple pie. It is an

urgent thing. This is something every girl should know in addition to sewing on a button and applying mascara correctly. Before I know it, I'm asking her, "If you had a daughter, what would you tell her?"

Mrs. Dupree smiles. "Oh, let me think," she says. "Well, I would say that every time you buy a new blouse or some wrinkle cream to make you look good, go and buy a book right away. It's just as important to keep your mind beautiful, don't you think?"

There is no one in the world like Mrs. Dupree. No one. A girl could learn a lot from her.

"Speaking of books, your friend Finn tells me you've been reading Ms. Lee's book," she says, her eyes staying focused on the dough.

"Yes."

"And what do you think of it?" she asks.

"I like Scout. And I like the town they live in. Maycomb. They walk all over town, too. I wish we walked more." I don't tell her how much Atticus means to me.

What I do tell her is how I wish we had a mysterious house on our block like the Radley place. The Stanley house with its overgrown wildlife is the closest we have to something dangerous, but that's mostly because of all the bees and bugs. If you used your imagination, I tell her, you could come up with something spooky happening behind those bushes. And then there is that stupid house with the plant sitting up on the dead stump. Much to my annoyance, it has returned, full of yellow flowers.

Mrs. Dupree makes soothing *Mmmmmhmmm* sounds as I go, which makes me want to keep talking. "Scout's a little like me, just having a father to raise her." But she had more courage, for sure.

"True. That's true. She is a determined young lady."

"I want to write to her," I say. "To Ms. Lee, I mean."

The rolling pin stops and Mrs. Dupree looks at me, through me. "You should, Sarah. People should never have stopped writing letters, even the ones they have no intention of sending. People should especially write those."

Mr. Wistler would like Mrs. Dupree. Why haven't I spent more time with her before? She is wonderful and kind, and here I am leaving. Maybe I won't leave forever. Just go away one year, become an anonymous seventh grader, and then come back as a whole new person.

"Would you care to help me with this pie, Sarah?" What I would care to do is curl up here and hide, read every book under this roof, learn every recipe she knows.

"Yes."

She puts a dishcloth around my waist, secures it in the pockets of my shorts, then stands behind me, laying her lined hands over mine, putting my palms on the rolling pin just right. I feel more happiness than a person can stand.

"You are a dear to help me," she says. "This one will be for your father, okay?"

"It's no trouble," I tell her.

"You are a sweet young lady," Mrs. Dupree says. "Raised up right." Saying this makes her cry, and so it makes me want to cry, too. "Oh, I'm so sorry. I'll cry over a turnip these days."

"It's okay," I tell her.

I know exactly how she feels. Another person in the house with you can make a huge difference sometimes.

We put two pies in the oven, and I wash the dishes while she sits and dabs at her eyes with a handkerchief.

"That sweet boy Finn reminds me of my son," she says. "He's a nice one."

"Thank you for letting me have the special book."

"Mr. Dupree would want you to have it. Because you *know* it's special. You know, I think we have a biography of Nelle somewhere, which would make a nice complement to your library, I should think."

Mrs. Dupree folds her handkerchief into a perfect square. "If Mr. Dupree were here, he'd know exactly where it is." She trails off, caught by the loss as if it just happened. I want to hug her tight in a way I've never wanted to hug anyone. I check my brain for the right thing to say, but all that comes out is "In your own words, what is interesting about her story?"

I sound dumb, I know, with Mr. Wistler's words coming out of my dumb mouth in this dumb moment.

Mrs. Dupree puts a finger to her chin and thinks on my question for a moment.

"Well, her relationship with her mother, for one. From what I understand, her mother practically ignored her," Mrs. Dupree says. "And her sisters saved her twice from drowning. Or so the rumor goes. Her friend Mr. Capote said that, but you just don't know about those things. People love a good piece of gossip because it makes them feel special inside of a minute."

Boy, do I understand exactly what Mrs. Dupree is saying about people. And now, of course, I want to learn about Truman Capote, too.

"The thing to remember, Sarah, is that Ms. Lee wrote a fine book, and that's what we know for sure. That's a fact."

Normally, I would stare at the floor, but I hold on to her warm gaze. I feel naked right here. This part of my life that involves having a crazy mother is not going to let me go no matter what I do. And the same is true for Dad. The news will always follow us. I am starting to think it might be a good idea for me and Dad to live in two different places. For me to move on. Sometimes in Westerns, two cowboys decide to split up and take two different paths. This confuses the person following them. It makes them harder to track, safer somehow. As much as I don't want to leave Garland, getting ready to leave is still the smart thing to do. I will have to research what Harper Lee did about her own family.

"Sarah, are you okay?" Mrs. Dupree asks me.

I realize I've been zoning out again.

"Uh, yeah," I say. And then, "Did she go crazy?"

"Who?"

"Ms. Lee? Because of her mother?"

"Heavens no, dear! What a thing to say."

"Stuff runs in families."

"Well, that can be true, but people are usually what they make up their minds to be, no matter who they came from."

I have a million more questions. My mind writes a list of facts:

There is another person in the world who survived like me.
She wrote a book.
She is not crazy.

She says, "I'll let you know when I've found her biography." But I am already picturing myself checking the biography out of the library the minute I can get a ride from Finn or Charlotte.

We sit together at her small, square table while the pies bake and the apple-shaped clock tick, tick, ticks. I am at least smart enough to ask her more questions about where she's traveled, let her talk uninterrupted so my mind can roam free for a little bit. How you can already miss someone when you are in the same room with them, I have no idea. But I do. I miss her right now, and I haven't even packed my suitcase yet. She touches that achy spot where my mother should be.

chapter 28

It's a Saturday morning and I am shopping with Charlotte. She wants new shoes to wear to Mr. Dupree's funeral on Sunday, but I know better. She wants to be at the mall so she can walk by Wilson's Western Wear and let the nonvaliant rake get a good look at what he's missing. She says they are broken up, but I'm not so sure. She's put on lip gloss and perfume, and you wouldn't get made up to go shopping with a twelve-year-old. Even I know this.

First, we go to Starbucks to get a double-shot/heavy foam/latte, though it's so hot outside I think this might have been a ridiculous/double-insane idea. Ha-ha! Charlotte says she must have black closed-toe sling backs, though I don't see why. She has a million pairs of shoes already but still wants more. I do not pretend to understand this about her. I yawn. Shopping is only fun if you have money, which I don't. She slides on the tenth pair of almost identical shoes and I nod my approval.

"So, what's the real story about Casserole Man?" I've been waiting to find out what happened behind the scenes and to see if Lisa's first-breakup theory is correct.

"I don't know. He has his moments. I'm not even sure I still think I'm in love," she says. "The whole chemistry with us is different now."

"Why?" I ask, which is a single-word question hiding one hundred questions behind it.

She considers a pair of silver sandals. The store lights hit them in full brilliance and you would think they were precious jewels.

"Well, I'm just going to play hard to get, is all," she says. "He cares about me and I want to see more of it." From what I saw the other night, there's nothing more to Christopher than a stupid jerk.

"He is just so in my face, you know. Wants to be with me. Wants to have his hand on my shoulder. Read what I've written. Talk about it over an espresso," she says. "It's all too tight like an itchy sweater."

This all sounds pretty peachy to me. Plus, you can always put a T-shirt under an itchy sweater to make it feel better. But since I know she doesn't want the truth, I leave her to her delusion, which is my new favorite word.

delusion *n*.: a false belief or opinion

It's clear that Charlotte is not the expert at relationships I thought she was.

Finn joins us at a square table in the middle of the mall food court. Their mother is coming home from her cruise tomorrow, so he is practicing staying out of her way. I wish the truth was he was there to hang out with me, but no, this is not so. I pretend it is true, though.

I eat a de-lish slice of pepperoni pizza and slurp my Coke, knowing how ungraceful it is, but liking the sound of it just the same. I think it is another side of me that isn't quite a real woman yet. Before you know it, Christopher has plopped down next to us and is all smiles. He thinks we've forgotten about his dark side.

"Charlotte, we're leaving in ten," Finn says.

"I'm ready now," she replies, and then gets up to throw out her trash. It doesn't dawn on stupid Christopher that he should leave now.

Finn leans back in his chair and gives me a wide smile that goes straight into my heart. I have to look at the floor or it will show. I find a mashed open ketchup wrapper and pretend it is the most interesting object in the world.

"Hello! Earth to Sarah? Are you still in space?"

"What? No."

"Good," he says. "I need your help. We have a mission."

First of all, I would never come to the Vikon El Bazaar Flea Market by myself, even though it is the strangest and coolest mall you'd ever want to see. For example, if you need a fake ID, a puppy, and a pullout sofa, this is the place for you. Finn has boxed up Mrs. Dupree's books to sell, and this is the place for them, too.

The whole building is a giant maze, and you'd better memorize how you got in so you can get back out. There are so many different booths stacked high with stuff, each one divided by a thin wall made out of white wood. The only thing connecting the shops are chains of multicolored Christmas lights strung up along the ceiling.

When you walk by the stalls, it feels more like you are on display. The salespeople sit in chairs, chewing on toothpicks, just waiting for you to admire a velvet Elvis or a giant pair of white-framed sunglasses so they can say, "How much would you want to pay for this?"

Being with Charlotte and Finn makes me feel confident enough, but I stay close because I am a tiny bit scared by how many eyes are on me. We each carry a cardboard box to the used-book stall. I browse the shelves while Finn makes the deal. I would stay in this tiny library forever, but Charlotte spots a vintage-clothing area and off she goes. We follow her and immediately it's as if we are inside an old woman's closet. There are at least five glossy armoires, their doors hanging open like wooden arms. The shelves are draped with scarves and beaded necklaces and brooches with fake diamonds. Shoes lined up on gold, mirror-backed shelves. An old woman's powdery scent is all over the place.

I run my fingers across a line of clothes. What if these dresses could talk? Did some beautiful young girl with bright red lipstick get engaged in this dress?

And the purses. They are in all colors and shapes and almost look brand-new. Whoever owned them either took good care of them or didn't go anywhere. My purse always looks beat-up and old, but not in the good way.

It comes to me suddenly how more of Mr. Dupree's things might end up hanging in this kind of store. Who would want them, I don't know. What do you do with a person's things when they don't live with you anymore?

Now Charlotte has found the mother lode of hats inside a giant ivory-colored armoire. We take turns modeling them in front of a long mirror.

Charlotte has a dark pink hat with a feathery plume coming off it. I have a classic black pillbox, and I know its name only because Charlotte tells me so. It doesn't exactly go with my shorts and flip-flops, but maybe if I had a simple black dress, I would look like I belonged back in time, standing on a train platform, waiting to be taken away. And then he, whoever he is, would step onto the platform and smile at me. Since I don't know what he would look like, I insert Finn's face into the picture, a blue suit matching his eyes so well you could see them across the crowd.

I tell my brain to knock it off and stop pretending I am a movie star. I don't know why my mind runs away with me.

Finn appears in the mirrored reflection behind us, swinging his arm around my shoulder. Something loosens in me and makes my neck go red. There he is in a gentleman's bowler hat, or so he calls it.

"You two are definitely going to be arrested by the fashion police," Charlotte says.

"Or start a new fashion trend," I say.

Finn decides we should all buy the hats anyway. His treat. He says hats make a woman look as pretty from the back as she is from the front. We'll wear them to the funeral for Mr. Dupree. *Go there in style to make Mrs. Dupree smile.* That's exactly how he says it.

chapter 29

It is Sunday and I am sitting on my bed, picking fuzz balls from my stupid pink comforter, trying to figure out why I am smarter than Charlotte. She had another fight with Christopher. Why would you fight with someone if you've already broken up with them is what I want to know. Still, I'm trying to be encouraging. I don't want her thinking I was a bad friend after I've gone, but even a blind man can see Christopher is no good. She is still suffering from delusion.

I tried to help. I told her the sixth secret of boys.

His actions will always reveal more than his words.

On the phone, I tell her to make a list of the hard facts about him.

I say, "When you write things on paper, it's as if your hand knows more than your mind. I don't know why, but it's true." I should know. I have two diaries. Plus, Mr. Wistler says so.

But now I have my own things to worry about. Does my private crush on Finn show on my face? I have to make a list of my own. He'll go back to school and in ten years we'll meet again at a bookstore, have a cup of coffee, talk about words, and he'll remember what a great girl I am and realize I am the love of his life. I already know he is mine.

The facts are right there:

- He knows my secret and wasn't mean.
- He loves the dictionary.
- I will never get tired of looking at his blue eyes.
- He bought me a hat.

I stare at my list while Charlotte complains into the phone, "He is just so clingy and has some personal things going on that, well, make him needy, which I understand. Besides, I have too much on my plate, so I think I'm going to break up with him." What I want to say is that she is *also* a little needy, but I don't. She might not tell me things about boys anymore if I point out the obvious flaws in her logic.

After we hang up, I am plenty distracted by thoughts of Finn, thinking about his arm around my shoulder. I can't wait to see him again. I try to read from Harper Lee's book until it's time for the funeral. This is my third time to read it. I am at the part where they have taken Tom Robinson to jail and a bunch of angry people demand that Atticus move away from the jailhouse door. The tension is so real, I can feel it in my bones. I am right there in Alabama, wondering what's going to happen next, wanting to shout back at those men to mind their own business and go home, which is sort of what happens when Scout talks to them. I don't know why I like this part so much.

Dad is pleased I'm reading this book again, and he says he wants to "make an appointment with me to discuss it over ice cream." Although when he sees it around the house, he gripes at me about keeping the book facedown, splayed open instead of putting a bookmark in its pages. I forget how much an old thing is worth.

The garage door screeches open, and I know it's time to go say good-bye to Mr. Dupree.

"See you later, Plant," I whisper. "I'll tell you a great story when I get back. Here's a cliff-hanger: I will look different when I return."

The funeral made me cry more than once, but mostly when I stood by Mrs. Dupree as she looked into the casket.

"There's my best friend, right there," she said. "Every

day when he left the house, he'd shout to me, 'Thanks for saying yes, hon.'"

She put one arm around my waist and hugged me to her. Then she dabbed her eyes with a handkerchief, a real cotton cloth square with an embroidered *D* on it. Even the way Mrs. Dupree cries is sublime, which is my new favorite word.

sublime *adj.*: impressing the mind with a sense of grandeur or power; inspiring awe

When I get enough money, I will get my own handkerchiefs. They will go along with my new woman status. Plus, I am wearing a pretty sleeveless black dress; my new, old black pillbox hat; and perfectly applied mascara, thank you very much. When I looked in the bathroom mirror, I saw a person who could almost be sixteen. Maybe seventeen if I had pearls and pierced ears. I mentally add to my travel list: get ears pierced. I might as well get in trouble for a bunch of things all at once.

At the reception, I hear Mrs. Dupree tell a guest about tomorrow's family-only burial for Mr. Dupree. I wish I could go, too, just to see him safe into the ground. I've never seen that part of a funeral, or any part of a funeral for that matter. I suppose I was at Simon's funeral, but who can remember things when you are two or three? I hope people said nice things about him that day.

Tonight the friends of Mr. Dupree help themselves to a reception in a wide-open church room with — you guessed it — casseroles. There are casseroles of every kind. Chicken. Beef. Macaroni. Mystery.

I collect bits of conversation about Mr. Dupree. If I add everything together, it all amounts to one thing: When you hear how people talk about a man after he's dead, you want to live an interesting life, give them a reason to say, "I miss that person."

Mrs. Dupree dabs at her eyes each time someone tells a story about her husband. Her handkerchief will be soaked at this rate, so I wish they'd stop talking. She is trying to be so strong. Her son, I've noticed, is pretty silent about it all, which makes me like him even less. He took his sweet time getting to Texas. What did he have to do when he arrived? Finn and I had all the books organized and boxed up, her garage swept, and Mr. Dupree's car washed, leaving him plenty of opportunities to come up with something good to say.

I spy Dad across the room, helping himself to sweet potato casserole. He is talking to an older man, pointing to a green Jell-O mold that no one has touched. He has been so secretive with behind-closed-doors activities and has forgotten to punish me for the Jim Beam. I am wary.

The room starts to smell of mushroom soup and face powder, so I step outside to breathe fresh air. The sun is at the point where it's painted a wide streak of orange and pink across the evening sky. I lean against the warm brick church wall, feel the heat sink into my bare skin. I close my eyes for just a second, letting loose my thoughts of Finn.

"Hey there," he says. I open my eyes, and it's as if he magically stepped out of my daydream. With the sun behind him just so, and his new bowler hat, he could be a movie star on a poster. I would buy it, hang it in my room, say good night to it.

"Hey yourself."

"Is Charlotte still here?"

"She left a little while ago."

"I thought I would tell her I was sorry."

"For what?"

"I sort of told Christopher to lose our address."

He takes off his hat, and the soft wind blows back his hair. Yes, he definitely has movie-star quality. I wonder if he would consider ditching his linguistic studies and moving to California. We could live in Mrs. Dupree's apple orchard, assuming his first movie made enough to buy it.

"She chooses bad guys," he says. "I hope you don't. Pick a good guy, Sarah."

His actions will always reveal more than his words. Check.

It would only be a few years to wait. Maybe less than ten. I'm pretty mature already, and it's not like he's an adult professional with a real job. He only delivers pizza in a rickety Toyota, so our real ages are closer than they look.

"Okay," I say. It sounds just right.

"My mother is back, so you know…"

"You'd rather be at a funeral. I totally get it."

He smiles, stares into the blue-pink sunset.

"So when are you going back to dictionary school?" I ask.

"Why? Are you ready for me to leave already?"

"No, I just want to know," I say. My plans to leave are flexible.

"Well, of course. It would be weird not saying good-bye. And I want a report back telling me you're going to read all the books I've given you."

"Sure." They are already on my dresser, lined up in the order I will read them. *And you be sure to take me with you when you go.*

"Sarah Nelson, you are remarkable in ways you don't yet understand."

What I wouldn't give for a pen and paper right now. I might even ask him to write it down so I'll never forget the line. *In ways you don't yet understand.*

I say, "Will I ever see you again?"

"Well, don't make it sound all dramatic."

I guess I must sound dramatic to all men.

"I'm going away, too."

"You are?"

"Yes."

"This is about your mother?"

"It's always about my mother."

"We'll keep in touch."

Keeping in touch is not enough. It is two cards a year and a wishing you a Doggone Happy Birthday.

"I think I love you."

Well, I can't believe the words came out of my own mouth. There she is, this different girl using my mouth, my lips, without permission. Maybe this is what going crazy is like. Maybe I have a split personality, too. All I can figure is that hearing people talk about Mr. Dupree's life gave that other side of me courage. You think about what you want people to know about you more than ever.

His gaze falls to the concrete ground, telling me all I need to know. For him, *love* is a trouble word.

He says, "Someday, you'll understand, Sarah, but you don't really love me."

"You know, you just said the one sentence I hate most in the entire English language," I tell him. "It is a linguistic cop-out for people who don't have an answer or don't *want* to answer. I understand a lot more than you realize."

He runs a hand through his hair, something I've pictured my own self doing, wondering how it would feel in my fingers. I love it when he does this. It's the way you know he's about to say something good.

"You are…unique," he says. "Unique. And since it's clear you are wise beyond twelve years, I will not bow to the linguistic cop-out. I'm sorry. So I'll just say that I'm flattered and that some boy is going to be very lucky someday."

He trails off.

"Vampires and mortals have the same problem," I tell him. "They can't do anything about their feelings except feel them and look at each other."

"Are you comparing me to a vampire?" he wants to know. I haven't thought far into this argument. In fact, I just pulled it out of my brain this minute. Of course he's the vampire, but I won't say it if it offends him to be the dangerous person in this relationship.

"That's not the point," I say.

I want to make him understand all he needs to do is hold my feelings. Never tell anyone. Just let them rest in his hands until I can collect them again, but no, he is not following my logic. I want to say how I've imagined kissing him, him kissing me back. I see myself being able to tell Lisa, "Oh, who did you meet at camp? Is that so? Well, I met a linguistics student. Nineteen years old. He kissed me and then I went off on my trip. It was the summer of my dreams."

I'm about to make the most intelligent comment of my life when you-know-who destroys my chance. My dad is so talented at ruining my life. Someone give him an award.

"There you are. Hello, Finn." He has a bit of green Jell-O on the corner of his mouth, and do you think I'm going to tell him? No.

"Finn just offered to drive me home," I say. "Would that be okay?" I feel bold with a capital *B*. If I die tomorrow, at my funeral they will whisper, *She was a girl who knew what she wanted, and wasn't it lucky she'd been kissed once?*

Truly kissed.

"If it's no trouble for you, Finn."

"He was going home already." I feel the fullness of my lies. They are dressing me up from head to toe.

"Okay, then." He kisses me on top of my head, and it's flat-out embarrassing right in front of your imaginary, possibly future boyfriend.

I step up to Finn, tell him I'm ready. I can't read his face quite clearly, but I know he's not saying no. He'll take me.

The inside of Finn's Toyota is messy in a neat way. Stacks of papers on the floorboard. Two bags of books in the backseat. Half-empty bottles of water in the cup holders. You can smell his cologne. He places his hat on the dashboard, puts the key in the ignition. The radio is set to a country station, the singer singing something about worn-out jeans and a broken heart. I hope the DJ says the name of the song. I must have it.

I watch Finn's profile, my favorite way to look at him. The sunlight has drained away completely. The moon is rising and looks to be about as big as a platter. If I had dreamt about this scene, this song, this dress, this hat, this guy my whole life — I would never come up with a better scenario than this one.

I cross my hands in my lap. I think I have all the necessary ingredients to make this happen, make this dream come true. This is something just for me, I want to tell him. Something a girl can keep in her mind forever. Just say it, Sarah. Say it. You're a woman now. You should be able to say these things.

A deep breath. He slows to a red light. We are a block from my house. I think about how I should say, *I want you to be my first real kiss, but not just for the kiss, but because it is you, Finn Reynolds. I've read it's important to carefully choose your first kiss. It will be the measure of all future kisses.*

"Listen, do you think what I'm wearing is okay for a date?"

"What?" He can't mean what I think he means.

"That girl I mentioned," he says. "This is going to be our first date. Should I change?"

218

"No," I say, quiet as a mouse. "That is fine." Nothing is fine.

I want to grab at my words in the air, retrace everything I've ever said to Finn, rearrange the thoughts so I would sound smart and he would like me. Why didn't I present my argument up front and then ask him? Appeal to the part of him that wants to succeed, tell him I must win this dare with Lisa, it is *my* time to be kissed, it can't be just anyone, because a girl will remember this until she's forty and old.

"I think I'd like to walk home now," I say. "Will you stop the car?"

He pulls the car over, leaves the ignition running. The glow from the moonlight makes us look healthy and nice. You would think this would make me less sad, but no, I am not. I am the definition of sadness.

"Sarah, I'm sorry." Why does it sound so much more beautiful when he says it? I don't know. *Sarah.* On his lips, my name sounds like a compliment.

"Thanks for the ride," I say.

Now he has an expression that isn't in the catalog of his expressions.

"I hope we are still friends," he says.

"I'd change that shirt if I was you," I say. "You don't want to smell like casserole. And don't wear that hat." It is the best I can do.

I will my hand to work, lean on the door handle of his

stupid old car until it gives way. *Slam!* The door is shut, the metal-on-metal crunch echoes the kind of scream I'd like to make right now, but no, I cannot. I can't let him see my tears. My hurt at letting him know all my secrets. *All* of them. The word *futile* surrounds me.

My face is streaked with tears. I told them to stay back until I got home, but they come unwanted. I wish I could see the pair of us from a distance. Him, in his car. Me, in my pillbox hat.

I walk down the sidewalk, hear my shoes clicking, stare at the full moon to guide me.

At home, there is a messed-up girl I see in the bathroom mirror, mascara all smeary and out of place. Her face red and full of despair. She whispers, *Hello, heartbreak. My name is Sarah.*

I lie fully dressed on my pink bed, tears sliding back from my eyes, filling my ears. I picture myself putting my love for Finn in my dresser drawer like a favorite shirt. Push it to the back. Forget it exists until it no longer fits. I would take it out a thousand years from now and say, oh, yes, I remember you. I used to like you, but now you are not my style at all.

Dear Atticus,
I want to start by saying I will never date a boy who has not read your book. I will ask them, and if they

say no, they can just keep walking. They are not the one for me no matter how cute they are. This could be a good way to weed out the ones with no brain, don't you agree? But hey, there is one boy I love who has read your book and I just can't talk about him. I am trying to be strong and not cry. I should change the subject now because he makes me want to cry and I don't want to cry in front of you.

So, new subject.

Right now, I am thinking about how you let your son, Jem, solve his problems after he'd gone and ruined Mrs. Dubose's flowers. You made him face the consequences on his own. So I know you would tell me to do the same. I have to go face the scary stuff in my life, which in a word is my mother. My mother. Ugh. I have to go see her for myself if I'm ever going to make you proud. I want so much to follow your advice about being in someone's skin, walking around in his shoes, and trying to understand. What I want to say is, why don't others have to try to see things my way? I guess I know what you'd say. You can't change others. You have to live with your own decisions.

If we were talking on your porch, you probably wouldn't say anything to me. You'd just push your glasses up on your nose and look at me. Yes, I know what I need to do, Atticus. Why is the right thing so hard?

For now, I've ripped out the page from your book that has your definition of courage. I know I am licked already, but I'm going ahead anyway. I'm going to take this page with me, then tape it back inside when I get back.

So this might be my last letter for a while. Please do not forget me. I am already crazy to write you so much anyway. Even Mr. Wistler would agree. If there is ever going to be hope for me, I should start writing to real, flesh-and-blood people. But I can't give you up.

Thanks for listening.

Your friend forever,
Sarah

Dear Nelle Harper Lee,
My name is Sarah Nelson. I am 12, and I've read your book three times. I wanted you to know how much I liked it, especially Atticus Finch. You might think I'm weird, but I felt like he just walked out of the pages and is real. He is such a true person. No one else fights for the right thing the way he does. I feel like I know him. Not every writer can do that, I can tell you. I've actually written letters to him, but I realized

last night that those letters are really to you. You wrote him into being, after all. I have a lot of questions for you. I've read some articles about you on my computer, so I know you don't let anyone come up on your porch and sit down for a chat. I will have to just write this letter and see what happens.

You should know right off that I am like every other nosy person in the world who is so curious about your life. I don't know if some stories about your life are true, but the main thing I'd like to talk about is your family. It seems like maybe our mothers had a few things about them that made them unlike most mothers, who have a million cookie cutters and pack lunches with heart-shaped sandwiches and little notes inside. I will leave it at that because I don't want to upset you, especially if all those rumors are untrue.

If you want to know, my neighbor Mrs. Dupree gave me her very own hardback copy of your book that has your signature. I promised her I would take good care of this copy. If my house catches on fire, I would rescue your book and my plant. Oh, this brings me to another question I have for you, which is, why do all the animals in your book have two names? I think I might be able to investigate this in Alabama without even bothering you. I could do a survey on the street and ask people the names of their pets. I think that is a good idea, and if I ever have a pet, I will give it a first and last name, too.

The last thing I'd like to know is rather personal, if you don't mind, but since you will probably never read this letter, well, I am going to put in everything I want to know. I wonder why you never married. If you are like me, it might be because there was one true person in your life and no one else was as good. That is the case for me. I would never get married unless it was to this one person, and that will never happen because he thinks I'm just a girl, which I won't always be and why can't he see that? Also, I read in your biography that you had a father like Atticus. I guess if you had that kind of father, any other person would be a poor substitute and that is why you had no use for a husband. I totally get that.

I guess this is all I have to say right now except thanks again for writing this book. It is my favorite book of all time and always will be. Thank you mostly for Atticus. I will never forget him as long as I live.

Sincerely,
Sarah Nelson

chapter 30

I dug the hole a foot deep. It took some trying to get through the tight, dry grass with a fork, but I did it. Then I used a serving spoon to shovel out the dirt. There is a good chance this spot will get water from our neighbor's sprinklers, but you can never be sure. It's hard enough to leave Plant behind, but thinking of her wilting and dying is something I don't want to imagine. I can't take her with me, because from what I can tell online, they might not let her ride on the bus. And I can't leave a note saying *Please water Plant*. Last summer when I was gone, she sat on the kitchen table and almost died of neglect. Every day he walked right on by her without noticing her obvious thirst.

I placed her into the hole and pressed the old dirt around her waist. Then, water over the soil. It should hold her for a while. I kneel at her new spot in the world and try hard not to cry. Tell her all the cool things she will be able to see from this view. The mailman. Sanchez Lawn Service. Little kids riding bikes. That little girl in white sandals.

I toss the fork and spoon into our bushes to hide the evidence and wash my hands with the garden hose. The dirt under my fingernails won't budge, but I'll worry about that later. I have to take the next steps of my plan. First, I'll ride the city bus for practice and then get a ticket for the real bus when the opportunity appears. In cop shows, as in life, you never know when you will have to make your move, so you must be ready. I begged Charlotte to take me to the Vikon El Bazaar, telling her I want another hat. She is game for this because she wants, what else, more shoes. Plus, I am planning to get a fake ID there with her help. I need one that says I am at least fourteen because that is the age you can ride a Greyhound bus by yourself. After I get the ID, it should be easy to pretend I am two years older, maybe even three if I apply the mascara just right.

The next step is telling my dad I am spending two nights with Charlotte so we can do plenty of girl stuff and suggesting wouldn't he like time to go out with PBroom?

My plan is working.

I cross the cul-de-sac with my purse full of money, my duffel bag packed with my clothes, my real diary, and Harper Lee's book. I tell myself it wasn't a complete lie. It's a soft one, like the ones he's told my mother about love.

The gentle, well-meaning kind of love. Because I wrote down my whole plan and knew Charlotte would never want to ride the bus on purpose, I had to do a small bad thing, a crime, really. I let all the air out of Finn's tires so he would have to take Charlotte's car to work. You should have seen the defeated car in front of his house.

And as long as I'd turned criminal, I decided to kidnap the potted plant those people kept putting out on their stump. I set it on Mrs. Dupree's porch with a note. She will take care of it.

When we arrive at the bus stop, there is an old man with a brown shopping bag. He looks so hot I want to do something for him, but what is there to do? He has to get somewhere and so do I. It's not as if I can turn on the wind. When the bus comes to a stop in front, he lets me and Charlotte get on first. I get a tiny thrill as I climb up the steps, scan the seats. Most of the passengers are traveling alone, faces turned toward the windows so you can't see what's in their eyes unless you stare at the grimy reflection, which no, I will not do today. I am not in the mood to talk to anyone except Charlotte. We need to be incognito. *Incognito* is one of my all-time favorite words because it can be a noun, adverb, or adjective. Mr. Smarty Pants someday-you-will-understand probably doesn't even know this.

As soon as the bus starts rolling, I casually tell Charlotte about getting a fake ID.

"I figure it's one thing Lisa won't have," I tell her.

"That is good. She won't have that," Charlotte says, and stares out the window.

On the ride back from the flea market, I stare at my brand-new fake ID. It's a good thing I need a haircut. My long bangs cover a lot of my age. I am wearing my new mascara. And I didn't smile at all, so I think I could even pass for fifteen.

Dad calls on my cell phone, and I try my best to sound relaxed and innocent of all my crimes.

"No. No. We're having a great time. Just doing girl stuff, you know. Talking about bras and shoes." I throw him off by adding just the right detail.

What do you know. Events change and my plan falls apart. There will be no getting out of Dodge, as they say. Gramps fell and broke his hip. He's in the hospital. We'll go down to Houston tomorrow to help Grandma.

He says to just come home from Charlotte's this afternoon, please.

"Morning, kiddo," Dad says. I am at the computer, trying to get a new bus schedule, and I might be busted.

I turn and see him watching me. He has his *#1 Dad*

mug of coffee. Ha-ha! What a joke that is. Why it hasn't broken in all our moves, I have no idea.

I'm caught. There's no magic pulley system to hoist me up through the roof. The evidence is on the computer. I feel dizzy and sit carefully in the computer chair.

"Just sending an e-mail to Lisa. She's still at camp," I lie. It takes, because he just nods and takes a sip of coffee as I click out of the Internet.

"Better get your bag packed."

My bag is already packed, just for another reason.

"Is Gramps okay?"

"He will be."

"How long will we be there?"

"However long he needs, I guess."

Here I am, traveling a highway, the same one I thought I should be taking to my aunt's house. I would have been half-way there by now. The first thing we were going to do was investigate the truth about Harper Lee's life. Research was at the top of my list. Aunt Mariah would know how to do this. But no, I am not getting an adventure. In Dad's car, the windows are rolled up, the AC is on full blast, and the radio is on some talk station featuring a host bent on making listeners as angry as him. I let my iPod wires hang by my side, have my feet up on the dash, slink down into the seat. It's a march toward sadness. There's no thrill waiting at the end.

I get bored of my music, even Finn's two songs, and pick up *To Kill a Mockingbird*. I beg Atticus to tell me something new and wise. If this was not such a special book, I would mark sentences with my yellow highlighter. I'm waiting for the day this feels like my own copy, like it was given only to me. Then I can call her Nelle like her friends do. Her biography says Nelle is Ellen spelled backward, which is her grandmother's name. You have to wonder if her mother expected her to be the opposite of her own mother.

Somewhere along the way I fell asleep, and now I wake to the sound of our car driving on gravel. I rub my eyes and look out the window. It's a Dairy Queen, which Dad knows is one of my favorites. Of all the things Garland lacks, at least it has a Dairy Queen. I slide my flip-flops on and get out of the car.

"This. This makes you happy, huh?" Dad asks.

"Why? What?"

"That's the biggest smile I've seen on you for a while." Well, they do have the BeltBuster and now that I'm here, I realize how much I need a cheeseburger.

We sit in a booth near the window, a tiny white vase with a lonely flower is all there is for decoration. The table has a red-and-white-checked vinyl tablecloth of the kind you might take to a picnic. Dad goes to the men's room, and I look around the place, spying only a few people.

There's a family at one table: a mom, dad, and two toddlers who won't sit down. They have ice cream dripping down their chins, and their mother reaches over, catches one by the arm, and wipes it clean away.

It's noon. After church, people start coming in, ordering their cheeseburgers and Dilly Bars. Unlike me, they will go home to lie out in the sun or watch movies. They will have simple, uncomplicated Sundays, and I am so jealous of this I could spit. I will have hospital food, Grandma fussing over my hair, wishing her hands could be folding laundry or sewing or chopping. Now that I think about it, Mrs. Dupree was happiest when she was busy cutting apples. And my mother busied her hands making paper birds. Maybe this is the kind of old woman advice they give in *Good Housekeeping* magazine. I could write an article. *Three ways to keep your hands moving.* When I am ancient and seventy, I can tell you this, my hands will be busy writing.

Dad brings our food, spreads it out across the red-and-white tablecloth.

"You've been having a nice time with Charlotte. And helping Mrs. Dupree so much. And reading a lot, too. I should get you something special for being so good," he says.

I am not good. I was trying to make out with a guy and beat it out of town. And of course, my fingerprints are all over the stolen plant on Mrs. Dupree's porch.

"You didn't tell me about your date with Miss Broom," I say to change the subject.

"Do you genuinely want to know?"

"Yes. Spill."

"Spill? I thought Finn was guiding you on the better use of language."

Who cares what Finn's choice of words would be? But my mind does an instant search of my brain. *Tell. Reveal. Impart. Inform. Divulge. Communicate.*

I will be the only seventh-grade walking synonym dictionary. Maybe someday there will be a job for this.

"Disclose all."

"There you are. It was nice. She is funny. Kind."

"Did you kiss?" I ask. He smiles.

Then, after a moment, "No, we did not."

"How come?"

"We've only gone out for lunch between our classes."

"Did you open the door for her at the restaurant?"

"So I'm being interviewed," he says.

"Sorry."

"Okay, Inspector Nelson. I opened the door for her at the restaurant. We sat in a red booth. When we came out, I think there was a bird chirping in the tree. Perhaps a blue jay. Perhaps an indigenous Garland brown bird. Yes, that's what it was. Her perfume smelled flowery. I wore the striped gray shirt you gave me, which looked quite good. Not too much cologne, as you have advised me on many occasions. She wore jeans and a brown shirt with these little gold buttons around the neck. It matched her earrings, I think. I think it did. And she enjoys old, black-and-white movies and the same kind of music I do."

"Well, she's the *only* one," I say.

He must like her. He's told me this much only once before, and it was about that awful Deirdre.

"Oh, and we made another date," he says. "A date date."

"Don't take her to the movies."

"Why not the movies?"

"If it's sappy, she'll be embarrassed; and if it's an action-adventure, you'll be embarrassed. Dinner is best."

"You're an authority, eh?"

"I'm observant. And don't wear that shirt you got for a dollar." If shirts had a popularity contest, this shirt would be booed off the stage. It is that awful. Still, every time he puts it on, he thinks he's a genius because he paid only a dollar for it. Well, you get what you pay for.

"Thanks for the tip," he says.

He could invite her to dinner, and I could make them King Ranch Casserole. Then again, maybe not. It didn't work for Charlotte and Christopher. Sometimes ingredients don't go together the way you planned and you end up walking through Garland in a little black dress by yourself.

chapter 31

When people cover their mouths with one hand, you
know something bad has happened. You see this all the
time in cop shows and Westerns. The uniformed officers
ring a bell and *Wham!* the woman opening the screen
door draws her hand to her mouth. The sheriff rides out to
a farm where a woman is hanging clothes on the line and
Bam! she silences herself with her palm. Someone has
died and nobody has to say anything. It is the universal
sign of grief.

Dad has his hand to his mouth now. He walked the
whole stretch of the cemetery, past thirty or forty head-
stones, before grief found him.

I would give anything to know what he thinks when
he stares at Simon's headstone. If he wonders what it
would be like to raise a son instead of a daughter. Why I

survived and not Simon. Does he feel like Finn's mother? When he looks at me, does he think of my mother? I put my own hand to my mouth out of respect, then I place blue and white carnations along the base of Simon's stone.

I slip my hand into Dad's, squeeze it tight. The stormy look is there behind his eyes. One hundred percent chance of Jim Beam and Dr Pepper getting together later today. There's a bottle in the trunk, I know it. He's already replaced what Plant drank at home. It was behind his shoe rack, which doesn't he know I will see because he leaves his shoes all over the place and I am the one to bring them back to the closet. It didn't matter anyway. We were out of apple juice.

We stood there in silence, each of us thinking our own thoughts about Simon and how life should have been. I got the feeling we might have a nice conversation and a crack might open up where I could sneak in a few more questions about my mother. My brain lined up a list on mental paper. One. Two. Three.

If we weren't ambushed by a nosy reporter, I might have gotten the chance.

This is what happened.

He'd said, "Gramps'll be all right. Let's go visit Simon before we go to the house."

Well, we should have gone to the house and watched the news first, because there was something about what happened ten years ago, which was my mother's crime. Why people want to make news of this, I have no idea. It is not like a historic date they make you remember in History class.

A pretty woman in a black suit and leopard-print headband came running up to Dad, asking him questions. "Mr. Nelson, hello. Sorry to interrupt, but could I ask you a few questions?"

Her greeting made it only worse. Even I could see she wasn't sorry to interrupt.

"Do you visit your ex-wife? How is your daughter? Is she close to her mother? Please, this would be a dignified exclusive. Why haven't you ever given anyone your side of the story?"

How she got to be at the cemetery, I don't know. Was she staking it out, hoping we would be there? Did she know that Simon's grave was one of the reasons Dad couldn't bring himself to move out of Texas?

There were curse words sprinkled into the sentence, *You have the wrong guy,* which was pointless because we were at Simon's grave and who else would we be?

A bright camera flash lit my face. Now there will be a moronic picture of me somewhere. Dad jerked me by the arm and pulled me with him. I broke free and ran back to Simon, tucking a page of Harper Lee's novel under the flowers. I'd meant to read it to him, but now she'd spoiled it all.

Dad's anger made him commit a crime, too, because we drove at top speed like bad guys being pursued by cops all the way to my grandparents' house. I held tight to the door handle, wishing we were still at home, thinking this has been a bad week for the whole Nelson family and the law.

My grandmother should not see him this way. She has enough to worry about with Gramps in the hospital. Fortunately, we made it there, no one following us.

Of course, I could do nothing but eavesdrop and write out my thoughts in my real diary as they talked about Gramps and what had happened. I wrote that you would think people would come up with something more original to ask, but no, they don't. They use the same question as a sixth-grade English teacher, only they have a big guy holding a video camera shove a microphone in your face and ask, "Why don't you tell us in your own words, how has life been for you in the last ten years?" This is an ambush.

This is what I hear my grandmother saying in the other room.

"That's an ambush," she says. "They have a lot of nerve."

pacing. When he does say something, it's a
that rhymes with *duck*.

Should we call your attorney?" asks my grandmother.

"What for?"

"It's an invasion of privacy, not to mention downright insensitive."

"Attorneys can't do anything about insensitivity," he shouts.

Grandma puts her hand to her neck and touches her pearl necklace. "I don't know why we weren't prepared for this. But how do you know what to do?"

"I knew it was a risk going out there," Dad says. "I knew it was the anniversary, or whatever you want to call it."

"That doesn't give them the right to intrude."

From what I can see from my hiding spot on the stairs, Dad's face is about as red as a tomato. They've unplugged the phone and my dad has turned off his cell phone.

This is all because of the ambush. I looked it up, and it turns out, it's an interesting word.

ambush *n.*: an act or instance of lying concealed so as to attack by surprise

The whole idea of an ambush sounds exciting, unless you are the person being taken by surprise.

The wooden stair step creaks as I rise and go to my room. I write down all my notes. What I decide about the whole day is this: Sometimes I think these news people need a life or at least better ideas about stories. I'd be asking questions about what will happen ten years in the future.

But I guess it's important to the news reporter with the leopard headband. She wants to know what's happened to us. Sure, I would love Dad to answer a few of her questions so I'd know the answers, too. But they know nothing about Tom Nelson. Asking him questions will only make him close up on the outside and explode on the inside. And besides, if they want an interesting story, why don't they go ask my mother? She is the cause of all this drama. Go to the scene of the crime, I say. I have half a mind to take my own advice and go see her myself.

The drama is all downstairs, and the second floor is boredom city. So there's only one option. Snoop around.

I like to look in my grandmother's closet or in her bathroom drawers. I'll bet she knows the moment one dust bunny shows up, the moment one Kleenex is used, which is why I have to use extreme caution.

I pull open the first drawer. It is lined with white-and-purple paper. The same liner has been there forever but still smells perfumey. She has a white divider tray inside keeping each type of makeup separate from the others.

The lipsticks stand on end with their color circles turned up. They are organized from light pink to bright red. She even has a section with her false eyelashes stacked neatly in individual clear boxes. If you didn't know, you'd think there are several faces asleep there. I love how organized this drawer is, and it makes me want to clean up my room, make some of my things special and neat.

I move into her closet. The first thing you notice is the scent of old-woman's perfume. Baby powder plus lemons. The second thing you notice is about fifty-three shades of beige. Her clothes are arranged with the same care as her drawer, all the short-sleeved shirts together, then long-sleeved, then sweaters. It's a beige parade.

I trail my hand along the shelves holding her shoes, also ordered from light to dark. Then, I spot a cream-colored peep-toe pump with something behind it. It's beige, but a darker beige. I lift the shoes, careful to memorize exactly where they were sitting. It's then I see them. A whole stack of beige books, paperbacks. I pull one of them up, not so careful this time out of my excitement. Because if this is what I think it is — OMG, it is what I think it is! My grandmother has a stash of romance novels under her beige pumps.

I put the shoes back, but keep one book. A few pages are turned down. In my room, I'm careful to conceal the book inside *To Kill a Mockingbird*. I open the paperback to a random page just to get the flavor of the story, see if it's something I can imagine right away.

"*Lana swept angrily into her bedroom and sat at her dressing table. She began brushing her long blond hair. Then she noticed the open window at the same time as a man stepped out of the shadows. She didn't know why, but she was strangely attracted to him. Was it the light? Or perhaps it was the gentle rain, hitting the streets of London outside. Either way, she knew this would be a night she would never forget.*

Then, he stepped forward and called her by name. She let out a sigh of relief for it. Perhaps he wasn't a total stranger."

Are you kidding me? She's already attracted to him? He could be a psychopath? A stalker? Haven't these people seen the Saw movies? How can my grandmother read this? I start from page one. I have to see if this makes sense somehow. I doubt it, but I am determined to know.

I wake up to my grandmother standing over me.

"Why are you sleeping on the floor?"

"Um, I fell off the bed." I always sleep on the floor at Grandma's house. She makes the bed so good, I don't want to mess it up.

"Sarah, want to tell me what's going on?" she says in a stern, clear voice I haven't heard in a while. There are so many things I could be in trouble for.

"Well…uh…em."

241

She sits at the edge of my bed.

"You know, you can ask me anything. You can look at my things anytime."

I am silent, retracing my steps in my mind. How did she catch me? Did I leave something out of place?

"Please just ask permission first."

Then, she places the romance book on the bedspread. "Good job concealing it behind a classic. Your father used to do this with comics."

I want to ask her a thousand questions about what my dad used to do, but my embarrassment keeps me silent.

"These books might not be age-appropriate for you," she says, "but if you are reading them, you might want to ask me some questions about, you know, whatever…"

"Have you read *The Valiant Rake*?"

"What?"

"Never mind."

"Wash up and come downstairs for breakfast," she says.

She tucks a strand of hair behind my ear and says my name. Sarah. That is all. Questions line up in my brain again, but there's no place for them to go. I wonder if there is a limit to how many questions a person's brain will hold. It seems so.

chapter 32

At breakfast, there are blueberry pancakes, bacon, and bad news. You can tell from the way my grandmother says good morning and how there is no place setting for my dad.

"Where's Dad?" I ask. She loads my plate with blueberry pancakes, then takes her napkin and smoothes it across her lap. Without even looking up, she says, "Your father fell asleep on the couch while watching TV."

Well, I already know why. It is the same at home. Nothing is ever going to change. Will she speak the actual words? *Drunk* or *drunkenness* or *passed out* are all trouble words for her. She prefers *overindulged*.

"Unfortunately, he overindulged a bit," she says. "Would you pass the butter?"

Well, doesn't that just put a cherry on top of my life. I

am so mad at him I could hit something. You would think he would pull himself together in front of his own mother and his sick father. But no, he is bringing all his bad habits from Garland, unpacking them from his duffel bag, making a big mess.

"I would like to have some coffee," I say.

"Aren't you a little young for that?" she wants to know. No, I am not. I am trying to get my life going in a positive way, steer the DNA inside me away from alcohol and toward caffeine. I go into the kitchen, grab a mug, fill it full, and carry it back to the table.

"Sarah, you might be too young to understand this, but your father has a problem with drinking."

If I told her all I knew, it would change the shape of her face. It would be an entire paragraph of trouble words like *passing out, hitting walls, forgetting birthdays,* and *wearing mismatched clothes to work.* But I don't want to change her face. It is already wrinkled with disappointment.

"What I want to say is, I'm thinking of asking your father to go get some help in a treatment center of some sort," she says. "What do you think about that? You would need to stay here for a while."

"For how long?" I ask.

"Well, we'll have to see how things go," she says.

The summer is not even over and here is Problem 3 for me to figure out. You can try to hide one parent with a problem that sends them to a hospital, but not two.

My grandmother adds another pancake to my untouched stack and another to her own. We sit in silence, watching syrup inch its way into the blue flowers at the edge of our plates.

"We'll have fun." No, we will not. It will not be fun by any definition of the word. I am so angry at my dad.

"Oh, this is for you," she says, passing an envelope across the yellow tablecloth. "Your father said he forgot to give it to you."

I take a long sip of coffee and open the letter. Grandma will not like me reading at the breakfast table, but I don't care.

Dear Sarah,

What's up? This camp is SO BORING right now, but I have HUGE news. I have a boyfriend. His name is Marcus and he's so sweet. BTW—he's not the one I told you about before who only knew how to use the smiley face on his texts! Geesh! Learn a new emoticon already! New guy goes to the boys' camp and we had a joint event one night last week. He was one of the boys who knew how to make a fire, just like that. He is also the cutest boy you've ever seen, way better than Jimmy Leighton, I promise. Go check him out on my Facebook page. I just changed my status to 'in a relationship' and he did, too! The problem is, he lives in Tyler, so we will have to be long distance. I also have to tell you that I have finally FRENCH-KISSED. Don't ever tell my mother! I didn't text this because she is checking my phone now. She would freak out. It feels risky even writing it here to you. DESTROY this letter after you've read it, okay. Promise? So, it was kinda weird at first, but he seemed like he knew how and I just stood there and tried to do the same thing. That was the first night, but the second night, I was just as good, I think. I never knew I had this talent before and now I'm sure I do.

So, I figure if I have found a boyfriend and had my first kiss all the way out here in the sticks, you must have too since you didn't have to go to your grandparents'!

Oh, and Renee told me that her dad finally asked my mom out. I don't know if I think that's gross yet. Have you heard anything from her? Has she kissed Steven Ng again?

That's all now. Remember to DESTROY this letter.

And check Facebook!!

XOXOXO,

Lisa

Well, there it is. She has kept up her part of the pact and has had *two* boyfriends. I've gotten my period, been to a funeral, and my dad is drunk on the couch. How can a summer that started out so promising turn around, put on its sneakers, and leave? I have a theory, and its name is Jane Nelson Ruins Everything. If it weren't for my mother, my dad wouldn't be a drunk and I wouldn't be the girl with the crazy mother.

I pass through the living room and see him there, snoring and sweating. Normally this would be the time I brought him a glass of water and aspirin, but he will have to tough this out on his own. If I had a glass of water, you can bet I would just pour it over him. I should take a picture, let him see his awful self, e-mail it to PBroom. Ha! That would teach him a lesson. He is sloppy with his hair a mess, his face unshaved, his awful one-dollar shirt.

I stand over him, wonder if he will wake up and apologize to his own mother. It comes to me how much I all of a sudden miss Atticus, which is another sure sign I am going to go crazy. How can you miss someone you've never met? Someone you only think you know because they walked off the page and into your room? I close my eyes and see the movie version of Atticus, let my brain go there.

Hey, Atticus,

It's me, Sarah. I am in a new place that is the same as the old place. We packed in Garland, but everything came with us. Our troubles. Our problems. Well, that is not what I want to talk to you about. I was just remembering that Mr. Wistler's assignment said to be sure to include why we chose the character we did. To write our favorite thing about them. I know I explained this once before, but now that I'm standing here in front of my sleeping, drunk, no-good dad, well, my favorite thing about you is that you are *not* Tom Nelson. Believe me, I am not being too harsh. You know Scout said about you that you could make a person feel right when everything goes wrong. That is true. Thinking of you makes me feel a little better. You know how to say the right things, do the right things even if there is a big injustice around you. Right now, I see an injustice in front of me, and he is asleep on the couch, folded over into flowery cushions. What a mess. He is a father only because he has children, not because he acts like it. That is an injustice in my book. And my mother, well, you know why she is not a mother to me. So what do I have, Atticus? I have myself to count on and no one else. Except you. You are the one true person I know. I can always count on you even though you aren't even real. How sad is that? At least I know you will always be the same every time I open the book. So it's just me. And my book. And Plant, if she survives out in the wild.

Thanks for listening.

Sarah

"Sarah," he says. "Good morning, kiddo."

I guess I am like a zombie, sitting there with Lisa's letter in my hand, looking out into space. He has to say my name three more times before I come out of my head and back into my real life.

In my mind, I say *I hate you*. What I say out loud is, "You're making my life more embarrassing, and I didn't know it was possible to make it worse. I don't want to live with you. Nothing ever changes. You say you will be different, and you *never* are!"

"Sarah, calm down," my grandmother says, stepping up behind me.

"It's okay," he says. "I'm sorry. I will make this up to you, kiddo."

"Don't make promises you can't keep. I already have

249

enough IOUs from you. And don't call me kiddo. I hate that!"

Well, I am making a scene, being dramatic, but I don't care. Even Atticus had a courtroom voice that made you sit up and notice. I am using my own new voice. The words shoot out of me quick and sharp. I've never seen his face so wet with tears, but his game of being pathetic will not work with me. I reload my mental rifle and fill it with every complaint I've had.

"...and you always, *always* forget to take the clothes from the dryer and send me to school looking like a stupid raisin."

He gets up, places his hands around mine, but I jerk back quickly.

"Sarah," he starts. "I am at my end."

"The end of what?"

"Myself, I guess."

"Maybe it was all your fault. Maybe you made her crazy, and that's what happened to her, and that's why you won't talk about it!"

"Sarah!" My grandmother pulls my arm with more force than I knew she had. "That is enough."

Fine by me. I am finished talking to him forever. If a person can fold like paper, then he just did. He slides back down to the couch. I've seen the bad guys in Westerns. They always fold.

"I understand why you think that, but it's not true. Falling asleep and waking up were the hardest parts of the day. So I drank. There's no excuse for it, but that's why. I felt guilty for what happened, you know. And now, I do this damage..."

Damage, I think, is a fitting word. He is damage walking down the street.

All three of us stay there for a long minute until Grandma breaks the silence. Do I want to go to the hospital with her? Where will my dad be? I want to know. I want to be at the place he is not. It is decided. She and I will go see Gramps and then to a free presentation at the fabric store, *How to Turn Fabric Scraps into Fun*. Dad will drink a lot of coffee and research rehabilitation facilities that teach people how not to drive to the liquor store. It is hard to believe we are all related, we are so different. In fact, if I'd done the class Family Tree Project, people would say, "You are joking, where is your *real* family?"

chapter 33

Once Dad made me afraid to say things. Now, I have this other girl speaking for me. She is brave. She says things out loud. She sticks with her plans.

I am sticking with my plans.

I am careful to delete the search history after I am done. When Gramps gets home, I would not want him to see the Greyhound schedules from Houston to Wichita Falls or the way I used his credit card to buy a ticket. But what am I going to do? I don't have all my cash with me in Houston and I want to get this done. The bus leaves at 11:15 p.m. and arrives by 8:15 in the morning. I'll be there before they even realize I'm gone. A taxi will pick me up at the entrance to my grandparents' neighborhood. Gramps and I used to take a taxi to the mall just for fun. He said he liked being chauffeured around. I can't say

I'm not a tiny bit scared, but I know what to expect. I've ridden in a taxi and I've been to the bus station. I just wish I had my black pillbox hat. It would make me look older.

I knock on Dad's bedroom door.

"Come in." He's sitting on his bed, dressed and neat. All the morning washed off him. He's wearing one of Gramps's plaid shirts and it hangs loose on him. He says he found a place to go to rehab, it's only two weeks I'll have to stay in Houston and then there are meetings he can attend near Garland and isn't that a good thing, he wants to know. I tell him, "That's good to do for yourself, but I need you to do something for me." By the way I say it, you can tell I've capitalized the word *me*.

"Okay."

"I'm going to go see her so I can talk. Just to her. I have things I need to say."

"Couldn't we talk—"

"No," I cut him off.

"Maybe a counselor…"

"No," I tell him again. I want to cry, but the brave girl won't let me. "You are evading. Atticus says a child can spot an evasion quicker than grown-ups. You are supposed to answer my questions."

"Who? Atticus?"

"Atticus Finch," I say. I toss Mr. Dupree's hardback

copy of *To Kill a Mockingbird* at him. He barely catches it. I tell him, read it, you might learn something.

"We've done everything your way, and now it is my turn. I don't think I could screw things up any more. I don't need to talk to you or to counselors or anyone. There are some things I need to say to her."

"Sarah, she might not be able to understand," he says, and I say I know, but I have to do it anyway.

"You said you'd make it up to me, and this is what I want. Were you lying about that?"

He passes the test, because he says yes to my plan. He says he will go, too, but why do we have to take the bus when he can drive? No, I tell him. You need to buy a ticket for the bus, I already have mine. Plus, I can't trust that you will be a safe driver in your condition. This last bit seals the deal. I've used logic to support my argument.

I tell him he can't sit next to me and must pretend not to know me.

"It should be easy," I say. "With all the experience you have ignoring me." The knife goes in. I sense its painful stab as I step out of the room and I am not sorry. You have to tell people the truth.

The Greyhound station smells of diesel fuel and armpit. In the departure area I sit in a hard plastic spoon-shaped chair. It is the most uncomfortable seat, yet a woman and child across from me manage to sleep sitting up. I plan to act as old as I can and not talk to anyone. I sprayed on my grandmother's perfume and stole one of her beige sweater sets, which gives me the appearance of someone at least three years older than I am. I would have stolen a pair of her reading glasses to enhance my look, but they make everything blurry to me so it was no good. I left a note for Gramps, too. *So sorry we are leaving now. You know why. I will pay you back. I love you.*

Dad goes off to buy his ticket. All over his face, you can tell he doesn't want to leave me alone. I start looking around for the kind of person I will sit next to on the bus. Someone Charlotte's age would be good. Even better, someone like Mrs. Dupree. From what I can see, my choices are a girl with a screaming baby or an old woman wearing a roll of packing tape as a bracelet. What did I expect? People traveling by bus to Wichita Falls in the middle of the night are not going to look like celebrities.

The number for my trip is called and I am on the bus, seeking out a place to sit before you can say *french fry*. I can't find anyone who looks clean or even makes eye contact. So I sit in the window seat right behind the bus driver's chair. When he checked my ticket, I noticed his shoes were clean, so I know he is a detailed person. On a crime show I watched the other night, the lead investigator said to judge a man by the cleanliness of his shoes and his car. These are signs of a person who takes pride in his work.

A man in jeans and a yellow T-shirt sits in the seat next to me. He wears thick hiking boots. I hope he won't talk to me or look at me much. He smells of gasoline, but it's not too bad. He has a tattoo on his arm of a growling bulldog and the letters *USMC* underneath it. Good. He is a Marine. Gramps has a similar tattoo, only it has a black panther instead of a bulldog. I take this as a good sign for my trip.

I spy Dad's reflection in the window as he walks by, but I don't turn. He can worry about me from the back, wonder if this Marine is flirting with his daughter. At least he brought Harper Lee's book to read. I wish he had the paperback copy with all my circles and underlines in it so he could learn how to be dependable like Atticus.

When we are safe on the road, I open my composition book and write until the Marine is snoring. The growling bulldog moves up and down with each breath. I try to make a sketch of it on the page so I can have a souvenir of this trip. But it is no good. I am not an artist. I am a girl with notebooks full of questions.

Then I write to her, long and true, as I've never done before. She wants to know about my new self — well, here I am. Have a look. Read it and fold it into a paper bird if you want.

Dear Jane,

My English teacher, Mr. Wistler, told us to write a letter this summer. I've been doing that a lot. He suggested that we write to our favorite character or someone we wanted to meet. Well, I would like to meet you. I would like you to know me. It is weird that you are more like a fiction character to me than a real mother. I can only remember seeing you two times since you went away.

You wrote that you wanted to know about my new self. I am writing to tell you all you are missing and more. This is everything I would say to you if you were sitting across from me at our kitchen table. You have missed out on a lot of things.

For example, if you were here, you would have picked me up from the car line at the end of the school year like all the other moms. We would have gone out and had ice cream at Sonic, sitting outside on those red plastic seats that leave criss-cross imprints in the back of your legs. You would have ordered chocolate and shared yours with me, too. I would have told you about Mr. Wistler's assignment, and you would have been excited.

If you were here, you'd know I want my birthday to be the opposite of what it is, maybe having a three-layer ice-cream cake and a pizza-party sleepover with two girlfriends, and you coming in with bowls of popcorn and Coke in glass bottles and a stack of *Seventeen* magazines and not worrying if we don't go to sleep until four a.m. You'd understand that it is so hard for me to get the birthday cards you send, to hold something that only days before your hands were touching, too.

Did you know I used to look for Simon's name on the back because it just seemed like something you would do? You might write his name last minute and tell me something wonderful you remembered about him. Or you might simply say, I'm sorry, which I've never heard you say, but I think I know that you are.

Also, you would know that I've had to become a liar. I will lie about anything for practice so that when I lie about you it sounds genuine. Some days I say to myself that my parents are divorced and that you moved to Paris to learn to cook and make up recipes with my name in them. My favorite is Sarah à la mode. Some days I lie and say you died, but that before you did, you made me a new Easter dress every year and let me pick out the fabric from the store. You bought enough to make yourself a headband, and so everywhere we went, we'd have a little bit of the same pattern on and people would know we were moth[er] daughter.

If you were here, my room would embarrass you. You would yell at me for throwing my laundry on the floor. You'd buy me a blue-and-white hamper that smelled of lavender and say would I kindly put things inside it, is it too much to ask? We'd argue, and I would slam the door and wish I could be left alone already. Then I might feel a little bit bad about arguing with you, but I'd be sure I was right. It's my room, I can keep it messy if I want to.

If you were here, you would always be brushing my hair, wrapping it in a warm towel, and telling me what kind of conditioner to put in it to keep it pretty. You would know how to make it just right in a nice braid or how to flat-iron it smooth as a ribbon. You would have known all about how to care for it when I got lice in the second grade instead of having Dad do all the work, which was horrible. Men do not know how to comb out a girl's hair.

If you were here, you'd have taken me out to dinner at a fancy place with cloth napkins. We'd talk about periods and ear piercing and boys. You'd say we're going to the super club store, and we'd buy a year's supply of products so I wouldn't have to ask anyone for help.

If you were here, the media wouldn't think of you as a sick person in a hospital. You would just be someone's mother trying to choose the right kind of peanut butter, adjusting your bra strap in the checkout line, and thinking about whether or not to make two birthday cakes for your twins or just one big one to share. I've always wanted to have two.

If you were here, I would have normal problems like pimples and sneaking too-short shorts to school in my book bag and wanting to have a thong show above my jeans, which I only want to do because other girls do, not for the comfort of it. Then we'd have huge fights about me wanting to stay out late at Jump Town because all the other kids do and why can't I? And the next day, you would ask me *my* opinion about a stolen painting you heard about on the news and my anger toward you about clothes would completely evaporate because who cared. You thought of me as someone with a brain after all. And then we'd make plans to go to the museum to look at other paintings, and you'd tell me you didn't think it was right for people to own art, it somehow belongs to the world like clouds and rain.

If you were here, I would know about Dad in your own words. What Dad will tell me every once in a while, after I've frustrated it out of him, is that he loved you very deeply. That you weren't always sick and in need of hospital care. It's still hard for him because he feels he still loves that person he used to know. It's not like you died, but as if you moved away and wouldn't tell him where.

If you were here, I wouldn't worry about being like you. I would have hard evidence about who you are so I could say, oh, this is the difference between Sarah and Jane. We are alike in this way, not so much in this way. As it is, I have to learn all of this on my own, don't I?

I'd like to hear your voice. I feel like Atticus, headed for the courtroom to defend poor Tom Robinson. (Do you know this book?) Atticus Finch knew he wasn't going to win, but he did it anyway. That's why I'm riding a bus to see you.

Well, I think I've said everything even though it is pointless. I am about to see you in person. Maybe I can say some of these things if I keep my courage up. I've learned that you have to choose courage each day like you choose what shirt to wear. It is not automatic.

Your daughter,
Sarah

chapter 34

The Wichita Falls bus station is full of people ready to go someplace else. The tattooed Marine runs across the lobby, throws his arms around a blond girl, picks her up, and swings her around. It is the sweetest thing. Someday I want this to happen to me. Someone so excited to see me they have to lift me off my feet.

We call the number for a local taxi service and wait outside the station to be picked up. I freshen up, brush my hair, eat a Tic Tac. Dad sits on a bench. We don't talk. That is our agreement. He called ahead and told them we were coming. That is all I need from him.

The taxi driver arrives and gives us an *are you sure?* look when I tell him the address. Yes, we are sure.

After we go through hospital security, a guard tells us to sit in the waiting area, and again I wait for a long time.

I flip through magazines, and Dad studies the carpe There is a woman working behind the registration desk now, and she calls for us.

"Family of Jane Nelson," she says.

I step up to the desk before Dad can speak.

"I'm her daughter. I'm Jane Nelson's Sarah. Sarah Nelson." This is the first time in my whole life I've said out loud that I was Jane Nelson's daughter. It just came out as natural as you please. The woman doesn't flinch. She's used to being around crazy.

She hands us badges to wear on our shirts.

She says, "Dr. Block will be with you soon."

There are no fashion magazines here, all business. So I stare at a TV mounted to the wall. The news reports on a line of three hurricanes headed toward the Gulf Coast: Igor, Julia, and Karl. A large chunk of Texas should expect soaking rains. This will be good for Plant. I miss her.

"Mr. Nelson?" I turn toward the voice. It is a nice-looking man in wire-frame glasses and a white doctor's coat, but I shouldn't judge him based on his looks. He might as well be a mad scientist come to study my brain.

"Thanks for seeing us," Dad says. "It was important for Sarah to just see her, if possible."

"No," I say. "Not if possible. I have to see her."

Dr. Block leads us into his office. We settle into two orange chairs facing his desk.

e to know you want to see her, Sarah," Dr.
"She's on medication, you know."
Yes, I say. "How is she?"

The way he smiles and clasps his hands together
makes me know he's glad someone finally asked. "Well,
you know this was a difficult month, with the timing of
the anniversary."

"I've written her a letter," I tell him, patting my backpack. "I need her to have it."

"It would be better if I had told her you were coming a
few weeks ago. Then she could have prepared for it," he
tells us. "She's aware of how ten years have passed, which
is one of the reasons she's more fragile right now."

"She doesn't need to say much. I just need to see her,
give her my letter. She doesn't need to talk so much.
Maybe if she just waved to me." I tell myself not to let my
courage dry up and leave. Did I come all this way to settle
for a wave? For just a glimpse? No, I did not.

Dr. Block exchanges a look with my dad, who has
remained true to his word, letting me make my own case.

"Wait here a few minutes, Sarah."

There is a flutter in my stomach, a lump in my throat.
The divided feeling is with me again. A tiny part of me
wants to run out of here as fast as I can. A bigger part
knows that if I leave now, I will regret it forever. The want

to run and the need to stay fight it out inside me. This is how Atticus felt for certain.

We've had to wait twenty minutes for Dr. Block to return, which is a pure eternity. Now, there is a fist in my chest, pound, pound, pounding. I tell myself to calm down. I'm at a hospital. If anything happens, they can take care of me. Bury me in the black dress and pillbox hat. It will make Mrs. Dupree even more depressed to attend two funerals in one month, though, so I can't die now.

Dr. Block leads us to a large glass atrium that overlooks a wide green lawn like the one I remember from years ago.

"She's sitting over there having breakfast by those white tables. Do you see?"

I follow the line of his arm. I see a woman in blue pants and a blue shirt in the distance, the space of a football field. It is close, but not too close. She sits at a white iron table. A gray curtain of hair hangs around her face. A breeze blows it back, and I can see the shape of her face. I'd like to pull her hair back, secure it with a shiny barrette. It might make her look more hopeful. She sits there, statue still. I put my hand to the glass. I can cover her up completely with the palm of my hand like the moon behind my thumb. But it is still as if I'm viewing something under glass. What I'm thinking is, I didn't come this far just to look through a glass. I could do that at home.

I ask to go outside, and Dr. Block says yes, we can, but all we will do is look. He thinks the conversation should take place another day. Give her time to adjust.

We go outside, all three of us. My heart pounds so loud, I pray she'll hear it, receive the mental thoughts I am sending her. *I'm right here. I wrote you a letter. Look at me. Look at me.*

She does nothing, just sits, sips from a coffee cup.

Turn! Turn! Turn! See me! I'm right here. I just want you to know I was here without me saying anything.

And then, she does. She turns her head. She's looking in my direction. Her neck and head are definitely pointed in my direction. I wonder if she will wave, but she doesn't. She is still. Calm. A stronger breeze blows my hair back. I see a gust swing her hair back, too. I was right. It would look nice pulled back in a barrette. I take out the camera I borrowed from Grandma, snap the picture. I don't even ask permission as I imagined I would have to do.

I step off the concrete patio and onto the green grass. I'm not supposed to do this, but still I go forward. Let me get in trouble later. But let me do this my way. I start walking faster, toward her.

"Sarah," Dr. Block calls. "Come back." But I am moving. Moving as if something else is pulling me. It is that

266

bigger part that has the courage. It is telling the small voice inside me to sit down, be quiet. Now, I am moving toward her, the long blades of grass sweeping across my sandaled feet. I don't have a plan. I take the pages of my letter out of my backpack and hold them, offer them.

They are in my hands, my secret thoughts. I want more than anything for her to have them so she can know me, a part of me. The good part that does not lie. Tell me she read the same book once, wanted to name me Scout but Dad was against it.

I stop walking. What next? I don't know. This is as far as my plan goes. Dr. Block follows me. There is an equal span of green grass ahead of me. What do we look like to strangers? Normal? Not two people involved in a crime. People who are talked about on the news.

It comes to me that I want to cry a pillow-soaking sob and then sleep at my grandparents' house, on the bed, under the covers this time. Hide from everyone in a safe place. But my legs won't move, forward or backward.

We are not together, but we are not apart. I could ask her a million questions or I could say nothing. It is my choice. I am smack in between. If I stay here long enough, they will have to bring me food. Cover me in a blanket. Bring me an umbrella if I need it. How long can a person live on a single piece of lawn?

Dr. Block is a few feet behind me, asking me to come inside and talk. His voice is calm and friendly. Okay, I say.

This is not the kind of variety I'd been thinking about getting this summer. Well, what did I expect? And there's no telling how many different ways you could describe how confused I am just now. I won't even let my brain go into synonym mode. If Finn were here, I'd tell him to shut up. And then I would want to hug him even though he wouldn't want me to.

I look back once, see her standing, talking to someone. Someone else gets her words and I do not. It is so unfair. She presses the fabric of her shirt smooth just like I do. But something about the movement makes her appear beautiful and tender. I want another picture of her walking. Later, when I print out the photo, it will show two friends going for a walk, talking about what flowers to plant this summer. As if this setting is a giant backyard they've worked hard on to enjoy its blooms. Two people just going for a walk. Normal. I bring the camera up to snap another picture. As I do, I forget about my letter and the pages slip from my hands. The wind whips them into the sky. My thoughts. My secrets. They are lifting into the gusts like freed white birds.

My feet move, running after them, stomping one page under my foot as it touches the grass. Another teases me and takes flight as soon as I get to it. The last page flies into the air, catches in a tree. The divided part of me screams in my head. *I don't care. I do care. I don't want to care about what people think anymore. I am terrified about what people think.*

"Let's go now," Dr. Block says. "I will get someone to gather those for you." He is so nice. I could hug him.

I am in Dr. Block's office, biting my tongue to keep the tears from coming. He's placed my bent pages in a neat stack. How he got them, I have no idea.

"Do you have any questions?" Dr. Block asks. It would be easier if Dr. Block could examine my brain and look inside at all the questions I have. There would be a new news story about me. *Texas Girl's Brain Holds World Record for Questions.*

I say to Dr. Block, "Tell her I came to see her."

"I will."

"She turned her head to me, didn't she?" I ask.

There is Dr. Block's gentle smile again. "You are not what happened with your mother, you know."

I let the thought tumble around in my brain until it sticks like a handle on a suitcase. I know I'll pick it up again and again. Feel it solid in my hands.

Dr. Block says, "It's just me and you now. You can ask me anything. Tell me anything, okay?"

"Thank you. You've been kind," I say. It sounds mature, like I knew it would. "Do you think I scared her?"

"The truth? I think she probably did not see you."

Well, it's not like I could have a normal face-to-face meeting with her. Not really. I couldn't ask her questions for a Family Tree Project. Find that one thing we have in common. You can't force someone to be your mother if she is sick. You have to lean on your own self. This shouldn't surprise me right now, but it does. All this time I thought I was so bad off, but now I see she probably has it worse.

"I just have one more question," I say to Dr. Block. "Why do I only ever get two cards a year from her?"

"It's complicated, you know. She's a bright person, but she feels she must never see her family again. What you have to understand is that just because a person has a mental illness, it doesn't mean that they are not very intelligent. For her, it's sometimes too painful, too destructive to remember because she understands what she did was so wrong. I know she wishes it were different. In a way, I think she believes she's protecting you."

We sit silently for a few minutes and it feels good, like I can catch my breath after running for an hour.

"There is one thing."

"Yes."

"I think someone should brush her hair back and put a barrette in it. It would look pretty that way."

"Yes. Of course. Thank you for suggesting it." He opens

270

the file on his desk, takes his ballpoint pen from his pocket, and writes it down. *Barrette for Jane.* Or so I imagine.

I will send her a barrette for Christmas. Maybe two. Lisa and I can go to Claire's and pick them out. No pink. Blue. Blue is her color.

"Kiddo, are you okay?"

My whole body rushes with adrenaline as I turn to see him, his arms already open, his eyes full of the kind of tears that do not fall. We have that in common, he and I. He throws his arms around me, lifts me off the ground, and spins me around. And it is me who cries, not him, as I hug him as tightly as my arms will allow.

"I'm sorry for what I said to you," I tell him.

"I'm not," Dad says, kneeling on one knee. His eyes meeting mine and telling me all is forgiven.

Dr. Block shakes my father's hand, and my father thanks him.

As we leave, Dr. Block picks up the stack of pages. "Do you want to leave these here?"

I had wanted to give them to her, explain what I mean, see her face as she reads it.

"Yes. I want her to have it."

"Honestly, I'd have to read it first. Is that okay?" You would think this would be the worst thing to ever happen, but no, it is not.

"Okay," I tell him.

There is another yellow taxi waiting for us at the entrance. The rain is pouring down now. I feel light. It is strange to think you don't know you are carrying a giant weight and you didn't know how heavy it was until it's gone.

Dad has his hand to his mouth. Grief is there. I lean into him, and he tucks my hair behind my ear with his hands.

"Can I ask you something?"

"Yes."

"What did you put on Simon's grave?"

"A page."

"From the book?"

"The part where Atticus describes courage. What it means to have it."

Dad tells me I'm the most courageous person he's ever met. It goes straight to that secret place inside me where I keep my favorite words.

chapter 35

Here is something else you have to learn on your own. Once you change one thing in your life, you can expect more changes. It is like pushing over the first domino. The others can't help but fall into place. If you are lucky, you won't mind the way they fall.

I am lucky.

I will have to reread my diaries to see exactly when the first piece fell. Was it the card from my mother? Or seeing her across the green grass when the wind blew her hair back? I guess all I know for sure is that my life has changed and I don't mind.

I stayed in Houston and Dad went to rehab. Then, back to Garland with my grandparents and Dad, driving the whole way without stopping, but I didn't care.

As soon as I came back to Garland, I exhumed Plant

(*exhume* is my new favorite word) and put her in a wide new pot.

exhume *v*.: to dig up something buried

Mrs. Dupree walked over while I was watering Plant and asked would I like some apple pie and to take home a couple of her own plants.

"I have so many from Mr. Dupree's service, and I can't possibly take care of all of them," she said. "We are both good with plants, don't you think?"

The next day, I hung out with Charlotte, who couldn't shake loose of Christopher and had to go through another breakup with him before she realized his being a jerk was more of a permanent flaw than a passing phase.

That first week back to Garland, I didn't see Finn much. He avoided his house because of his mother and said he was holing up in the library studying.

It isn't until today, when I climbed back up on the stump outside to watch Sanchez Lawn Service mow Mr. Gustafson's lawn, that I talk to Finn. I guess I am so distracted, I don't notice it when he drives up to our curb and rolls his window down.

"Why *do* you stand up on that stump?"

"Because no one else does it," I say, jumping down and

sticking the landing. I walk to his car, lean on the window frame. "Going back to college with your girlfriend the dictionary?"

"Yes."

"You'll be happy to know I'm completely, entirely, absolutely over my crush on you," I lie. "So you know, you can still send me e-mails and texts."

"That's good."

"We'll always have *The Price Is Right*."

"And hats."

"And Harper Lee."

"Speaking of hats, I have something for you."

He hands me a bag with his bowler hat inside.

"Keep it for me, okay?" he says, and I know right then I will have it forever. Let Lisa have her first French kiss. This is better.

When he drives away, I mouth the words *I still love you, Finn Reynolds*.

Then I put on my new favorite hat, skipped a rock down the sidewalk, and thought about calling Lisa and planning a trip to the mall. There is still almost one month to go before I have to face seventh grade, and my wardrobe needs attention. Maybe I'll just wear this hat when I present the dreaded Family Tree Project. I'm not completely certain about what my project will include, but now it feels more like an annoyance than a giant problem.

Anyone watching the news this summer already knows about my mother anyway, so I will just have to find my courage. I can say I don't know a lot about her and we are not close. The rest is none of your business. That is the truth.

Now, I go into the garage to get a nail so I can hang Finn's hat in my room. What do you know, the garage door screeches open and scares me to death. I hate this house. There is Dad with a big smile on his face.

"Where are the nails?" I ask him.

"What do you need a nail for?"

"To hang something on my wall."

"How about your *new* wall?"

"What are you talking about?"

And here is the next piece to fall that I didn't see coming. Tonight at dinner, Dad announces to me and my grandparents, "I bought us a house on Harvard. Two blocks over. All the walls are white. We can paint it whatever color we want."

Well, I wasn't expecting that.

He hugged me tight and then smiled all through dinner. I've never seen him smile so much. After, I helped Grandma clean up the kitchen, where she'd made breakfast for dinner, which isn't that a cool idea? French toast, maple sausages, and fresh fruit. She made our ugly rental kitchen smell sugary. I will make our new one smell good, too. There will be plants everywhere, with Plant, the queen of all plants, in the window over our new sink.

When I go to my room, I find a neat stack of washed clothes at the edge of the bed. This is something my grandmother has done. Washed my shorts and shirts and folded them all in neat squares. I tell myself I will do this at the new house. Take my laundry fresh from the dryer and fold it neatly, put it in my drawers from light to dark the way she has arranged her drawers and closet. Arrange my makeup drawers so they look like a fancy cosmetics counter, put scented paper in every drawer and cabinet, especially those containing my one year's supply of feminine products. Grandma liked my idea of going to the super club store and saving me the embarrassment of ever asking Dad to buy them.

I go to the kitchen to thank her and find her wrapping sandwiches in wax paper. I don't know anyone else who does this except for my grandmother. It is strange and wonderful at once, makes the meal seem gift wrapped especially for you. I think it's something I would like to do for my own children. She also has the ironing board out. There are signs that she's just finished ironing my dad's underwear. This is definitely *not* something I will do for my children.

"I always look forward to our visits," she says, with a

little bit of sad in her voice. I want to say, "You do?" But it isn't right to question her. "I talked to your father, and we agreed on something. Or rather, I let him know how I feel, and now he agrees. It's time for you to get your ears pierced. He said he would take you next Saturday."

She touches my shoulder, her hand trails up to my hair and hooks it behind my ear. "Little diamond studs would be nice, and they go with everything."

A surge of warmth and love comes up through my chest. I hug her, lean into her with the weight of my new-found happiness. I don't think she expected it, because her body flexes backward. She and I have never been affectionate. But there we are, two people hugging in a kitchen like it happens every day.

"We have to tell your father a few things about girls, you and I. He doesn't always remember," she says.

In my room, I put on my pajamas and sit on my bed. It is not my fake diary that I reach for now. It is too much work to keep up and so last year. I pull out my green composition book and open it to a clean white page. There are a thousand and one thoughts I want to write, some just for me, a letter to Atticus. And a letter to Mr. Wistler that might just have to say *Thank you for being the best teacher ever.* But the words won't travel from my brain to my hand just yet.

I keep thinking about how this summer went so fast

and I want to slow it down now. Pause it and replay it in places. The moment my lost pages caught in the trees. The way her hair hung around her face. The cracks of sadness in my father's heart. The boy with a thousand words who looks too much like his father. Me in a pillbox hat, coming and going. A woman's hands rolling out dough for an apple pie. And an old book that is more like a friend, somehow new each time I open its pages.

I feel exhausted, so I close the notebook. I know I won't forget to tell Atticus later that Mrs. Dupree found her old copy of *The Gray Ghost*, a story he read to Scout. We are going to read it together. It is silly to think it, but he would like that.

Dad pushes my door open a tiny bit and steps inside my room. "So, I hope you're happy about the move," he says.

"Yes."

He walks over and sits down on the edge of the bed.

"Good."

"Did you know that Grandma actually ironed your underwear?" I ask.

He nods and smiles.

"That is so messed up," I say. "You have to do something about it."

He pulls up the covers and tucks them under my chin.

"Well, what can I say, kiddo. We all have to survive our parents' imperfections, ironed underwear and all."

"But what if PBroom was to see that? How would you survive the embarrassment?"

He holds out each of his hands. "There's the parent you want and the parent you have. If you're lucky, sometimes they are the same person."

Well, I thought we had nothing in common. But it's easy to forget your parent is also someone's kid.

"Tell me more ways she embarrassed you?"

"That would take all night," he says. "Tomorrow."

He kisses my head and turns out the light. When we wake up in the morning, I know he will talk to me.

Acknowledgments

Every writer should have a supporting cast of inspirational, smart, and encouraging people behind her. I am lucky enough to have such a cast. I'm deeply thankful to the following people. My agent, Julia Kenny, for her wisdom, advice, and advocacy — and for making dreams come true. My brilliant editor, Bethany Strout, for her talent, grace, and cheerfulness. Special thanks to Alvina Ling and everyone at Little, Brown. I think this is the best team in publishing.

To my supportive and wonderful friends Kathryn Casey; Mylene Clark; Dave Diotalevi; Robin Gage; Cheryl Haase; Cathy Heape; Anne Hunter; Julie, Mark, and Katie Neinast; Jenny Wingfield; Sandra and Eldon Youngblood; and most especially, Amy Hazell. I am truly blessed by each of you.

To Kathy Patrick and all the beautiful Pulpwood Queens. Thank you for being a book's best friend.

To the memory of my sixth-grade English teacher, author G. Clifton Wisler. Sometimes just being in the presence of a passionate teacher can inspire you for the rest of your life.

Finally, thanks to my family for giving me the love and wide-open space to be creative. Foremost to Matt, who always believed, always encouraged. I love you. To Dad and Kathy, for loving me and bringing me brownies. And to Chloe and Molly, who put a smile in my heart.